THE WATER CATCHERS

Bhairavi was born in Nairobi, grew up in London and now lives in Mumbai. She works in the areas of Language Training and Education. Bhairavi is interested in all kinds of cross-cultural exchanges and the quirkiness and good-natured humour that results from it. This is her first novel.

Write to her at thewatercatchers@gmail.com and share your thoughts on the book and all things related to water conservation.

THE WATER CATCHERS

BHAIRAVI PAREKH

Illustrated by
AINDRI CHAKRABORTY

hachette
INDIA

First published in 2013 by Hachette India
(Registered name: Hachette Book Publishing India Pvt. Ltd)
An Hachette UK company
www.hachetteindia.com

SRD

ISBN 978-93-5009-684-0

Hachette Book Publishing India Pvt. Ltd,
4th & 5th Floors, Corporate Centre,
Plot No. 94, Sector 44, Gurgaon 122003, India

Typeset in Bembo Std 11.5/15.2
by Eleven Arts, New Delhi

Printed and bound in India by
Manipal Technologies Limited, Manipal

FSC www.fsc.org
MIX
Paper | Supporting responsible forestry
FSC™ C043100

FOREWORD

It is good to know that Bhairavi Parekh has written a novel around the theme of water. It is critical that younger generations in India understand that their future well-being depends on how we value and use water.

Today, we are in a very dire situation when it comes to water availability and its quality, for all the myriad uses we want to put it to – from critical uses like irrigation for growing our food, to hydro-power for electricity, and now to swimming pools and jacuzzis for aspirational lifestyles! Everyone in India needs to internalize the fact that the environment has first claim on water, for all the ecosystem services it provides us, and human beings can sustainably draw water only after that need is met. This means that we have to find better ways to fairly and equitably use our limited water resources 'quota' across urban and rural domestic needs, livelihoods, agriculture needs and industry needs.

Water is a finite but renewable resource. If we can renew our relationship with it, there is no reason India, with all the munificence of its monsoons, its many perennial rivers, its massive aquifers, and more, cannot become a water wise – and prosperous – society and economy. So let's do that. Let us, each one, renew our relationship with water. It's the right time!

Rohini Nilekani
March 2013

1

UNDER THE MUMBAI SKY

If you ride up in a helicopter and kick a football from it over the city of Mumbai, you can bet it will bounce off a building. That's because there are more than a million buildings there and not much space between them. Of course, it might whizz past one of the thousands of black crows that squawk across the city night and day. If it found a space between, it might bounce on the roof of a car, the top of a train, or finally, the head of one of the twenty one million people rushing to and fro in the city to find their dream.

Chintan's building was sandwiched between a new multi-storeyed apartment block and the local grocer who also had a photocopying machine and sold SIM cards for mobile phones. The lane next to the grocer was the regular haunt of the cow lady. She hired a cow for the day and slung a sack of fresh grass along the brown back of the cow. Passersby gave her a few coins, received some grass, fed the cow, took its blessings and walked on. At the corner of the lane, on the footpath, stood the wooden box of the rice writer. For twenty rupees, he wrote your name with the thinnest of brushes onto a tiny grain of rice, stuck it in a tube of oil and sealed it. Next to him, inside a wire cage, belonging to Abu Chacha, coconuts lay waiting for customers. This was Chintu's favourite spot. He could stand at this corner and view the whole street and its inhabitants as they went about their daily life.

It was about 6 a.m. and unearthly sounds emerged from the small apartment where Chintu lived. The sun's rays entered the house through the window over the narrow bed. They caressed yesterday's fading orange flowers placed in front of the picture of Lord Shiva, which rested on the old chest of drawers. The early morning sun gradually lit up the room bit by bit, wafting over the almirah and lighting up the patterns on the thin curtain that served as a door. It warmed the tousled grey head of his grandfather, bent low in prayers over a thick book. As soon as the rays of the sun fell on the book, the grey-haired man closed it, touched it gently to his forehead and placed it on a wooden stand in the corner. He slipped his feet into rubber slippers, smoothed down his white *kurta* and strode out of his room. After that, all hell broke loose.

'Chintya!'

Silence.

'Chintu, Chintya!'

'Groan . . .'

'ChintyaMintyaPintyaLalluBalluKalluTallu!'

'Mmnhngmm . . .'

It was 6.30 a.m. and Chintu was snugly ensconced under a light cotton sheet with the fan whirring above. He was in the middle of a happy dream about a day without his school, homework, or the dratted Sholay Gang.

'Chintan Vishnubhai Mansukhlal Shah, get up!'

'Mnnnngh . . . Dada, I'm not five years old anymore!'

'No, no! You are the eleven-year-old Formula 1 champ, Schumacher-Bumacher! Start racing, bathe, eat, pack your bag, catch your bus! You have fifteen minutes!'

'Fifteen minutes? That's all?'

'You'll make it! Remember I'm the best coach! Quick, into the bathroom! Zoom! Now!'

Chintu darted out of bed and zigzagged sleepily into the bathroom with its single tap, a shower nozzle and two plastic buckets.

'Quick, quick, quick!' shouted Dada from outside.

On such rushed mornings, he almost regretted following the Formula 1 races night after night on TV. Dada and he had been addicted to the sport. In their excitement, they would have spilled into the TV box and then into the racing action. The thrill of it! Car after car zoomed past faster and faster, Ferraris, Renaults, Mercedes . . . desperate crowds . . . the sound . . .

Ever since the first match they had watched together, Dada had appointed himself the Formula 1 coach of their household, supervising Chintu's daily routine with a virtual starting gun. It was fun, but terribly hard for poor Chintu to manage on school-day mornings.

'Have you finished your bath?' Dada asked through the door.

Chintu grabbed the bathing bucket and struggled with the tap. Oh no! Water cut again! He splashed the half bucket of stored water over his thick black hair, towelled himself vigorously and emerged.

'What? Just dry-cleaned again today? Shiva, Shiva! Soap your hands and face at the sink. There's some water in that bucket. Hurry!'

'Dada, when you pray to the Lord, do ask him for a jet plane in the mornings.'

'Hmm, you know jet planes always take off late these days. Better grow wings instead! Finish eating. Get your bag. Here's your lunch box.'

'Zoom zoom.'

'Put on your glasses,' said Dada.

Chintu slid the black-framed glasses over his nose.

'Here's the matchstick.'

Chintu took it, lit the lamp in front of Lord Shiva's picture, prostrated and grabbed his school bag.

'Did we beat the Formula 1 record today, Dada?'

Dada's eyes gleamed behind his specs. 'Of course! Schumacher uses my clock! Now go!'

A face emerged from the kitchen. 'Chintya, is all your homework done?'

'Yes Ma. Bye!'

'Waaiittt!'

Chintu swivelled round. Grandfather pointed to the laptop. 'The Internet. You reset the password yesterday! Now log on quickly before you go.'

Chintu smiled teasingly. 'And lose the Formula 1 race? Never! I can't disappoint my coach!'

He opened the door and took the stairs at a run. 'Okay, okay! It's your name—Mansukhlal Shah! That's the new password! Bye!'

He reached the main road and sprinted to the corner where Abu Chacha was sorting out his crates of coconuts. 'Chacha, how's the baby today?'

Abu Chacha patted his ball of a stomach swathed in a blue and brown striped *lungi*.

'Growling for its morning tea! See you after school.' Chacha's stomach triggered daily jokes between the two of them.

The school bus appeared, rumbling and rocking at the corner of the street. Chintu scampered up the steps, and was swallowed up into its noisy interior. He would be gone for the next eight hours.

Life began early in Mumbai. Sometimes, it was still dark when Chintan came down to catch his bus. Even so, he would find Abu Chacha, the cow lady and the rice writer, all ready to go about their daily business.

Every time he saw them, Chintan would think that one could make a living in Mumbai doing the most fascinating things.

What Chintu didn't know was that one could also make a living in this city by doing some very strange things. For example, the water shortage in his house this morning wasn't due to less supply from the municipal corporation alone, it was also due to a clever water thief in his neighbourhood!

Every morning, a municipal lorry drove up. It was a water tanker, delivering water to the buildings in that area which were plagued by shortage. The driver parked outside 'Vijay Drapers' shop and got down to unload the water into the official government cement tank. From here, metal pipes fed the water to the buildings around. On most days, a scowling man with a scruffy black beard came up to the driver, clapped him on the back with a lopsided grin and steered him to the corner tea stall.

'Driving, driving all day. What's the point of working so hard if you can't even have a cup of tea every morning, huh? Come on, it's nice and hot.' The man running the tea stall poured them two tiny cups while the scowling man talked away. 'What a great life! You work your backside off and what do you get? Not even enough money for a half-decent meal every day! Prices going up all the time, we need to change the government . . .' The tea stall guy poured another cup each.

Behind the tanker, the scowling man's accomplice had already sneaked up and connected two big rubber pipes to the two large taps on the tanker. He turned on the taps. The water flowed thickly out of the tanker through these pipes into a large rubber container hidden behind 'Vijay Drapers'. In seven minutes, while the driver was still sipping his tea, this container filled up. The accomplice pulled out the pipes, signalled to the scruffy man and disappeared leaving no evidence. The scruffy man stopped his complaints and steered the driver back to the lorry. 'Okay okay, you don't have to listen to my complaints early in the morning. What would the people of this area do if you didn't provide them with this water?'

The driver, who had been silent all through, just nodded. He connected his pipe to the official cement tank built by the government, filled it, removed the pipes and waved as he drove off. *Good,* thought the scowling man. *I can make some easy money again today. That much water will be worth at least two hundred rupees and all it cost me was a cup of tea. Ha.*

So while Chintu went to school, Abu Chacha sold coconuts, the cow lady paraded her cow, the rice writer wrote names on a grain of rice and the scowling man stole water! Many people never found their dreams. Instead, they spent their waking hours trying to earn a living in this city.

★★★

At home, Mansukhlal or Mansukhbhai, as everyone liked to call him, shut the door and made a beeline for the laptop.

'Reset the password, put in my name . . . there we are! And click to . . . hmm . . . Facebook!' he muttered happily to himself. 'Such an invention, this computer! And Chintu. Such a *gagdoo*, this boy!'

He smiled to himself. Mansukhlal was a whizz at making up names that meant nothing.

'Champion Coach, breakfast is on the table. The Internet doesn't provide food,' Vimla bantered. She had to leave for work.

'Ah, maybe one day it will! Such a wonder, the Internet is!' His eyes glazed over and his moustache quivered. In his vision, the laptop had begun sprouting his favourite delicacies.

'Vimla, I'll have my *poha* later. You go on to the office now. I'm at home today.'

'What's this new fad with Facebook? Are you chatting with your son?' Chintu's father, Vishnu, was on a year's contract, working for a pharmaceutical company in Dubai.

'Hmph! Does your royal husband, ever take his eyes off his office papers? His office chair must be falling apart due to wear and tear!'

She laughed. 'Ah, so then you have some secret search on the Internet!' She picked up her handbag.

Mansukhbhai looked up. 'Yes. I'm on a quest.'

'What?'

He took off his glasses and polished them on his white *dhoti*. 'I was going to tell you all sometime soon.'

'Hmm.' Vimla was startled at the change of tone. Her father-in-law could be very dramatic if he wanted to be, but this time he looked serious. She looked at her watch and stopped herself from asking more. She would be late for work.

'Okay. We'll discuss this after dinner? Chintu's back at 4 p.m. There's *thepla* and milk for him, then he can go downstairs to play, but he must finish his homework by 6 p.m.'

They finished the last part together. The chant rarely varied.

'I'll be back for dinner. The food's in the fridge in case you're hungry early,' she added.

Mansukhbhai returned to an easy banter with his daughter-in-law. 'Chintu's getting smarter . . . next year he will outsmart me. Then you will have to take over his homework!' he teased.

Vimla called out from the door. 'Yes, then you can start cooking!' Her laugh rang out as she shut the door behind her.

Mansukhbhai was very proud that his daughter-in-law had a job. The other elders of the community said all kinds of things about wives that worked in offices. *Her husband doesn't earn enough. She doesn't want to cook and clean.* Mansukhbhai kept quiet through their comments as he was quite satisfied with the way things were in his own house. He could look after Chintu till Vishnu returned from his year's work assignment in Dubai.

After breakfast, Mansukhbhai returned to the computer. Over the last couple of weeks, he had turned into an Internet geek. Every afternoon, he would hunch over the new laptop that his son had bought him and surf the Internet for hours.

Mansukhbhai would sit on his favourite chair with his long white *dhoti* tucked under him. This length of cloth, tied at the waist, hung in folds down to his leather slippers, partially exposing his brown calves. Chintu was mortified whenever his Dada wore his *dhoti* and made one of his rare visits to Chintu's school.

'Dada,' he would protest. 'Can't you wear a pair of trousers? All the other fathers wear trousers!'

'First, I am your grandfather and second, I haven't owned a pair of trousers for the last fifteen years.'

'Then it's high time you bought some!'

'Okay. Let's go. Where can we buy air-conditioned trousers?'

'What do you mean?'

'Like this *dhoti*.'

'Dada, what are you talking about?'

Grandfather bent down and pointed to where the thin *dhoti* parted at the calves. 'Look! It is air-conditioned!'

Chintu groaned. Trying to convince Dada about something was like batting a googly ball: you never knew at which angle the ball would bounce off. But there was always an invisible bag of laughter around him. No. The *dhoti* would stay. Dada had decided. He said that his father had worn a *dhoti*, and his father before that. He was the last in the line of Shahs, who tackled the world with their *dhotis* firmly tucked in place!

As Mansukhbhai got engrossed in his computer, the eternal noise of the Mumbai traffic, the raucous calls of the vegetable vendors and the watchman's loud laughter slowly melted away. He sat immersed in the mission at hand.

'Bhailalbhai Shah . . . born in Tintodan, Gujarat, in 1951. Married. Two children. Have to study his profile now. I wonder . . .'

Suddenly there was a gurgle, then a whoosh of water as the taps came alive again.

'Oh Shiva, Shiva! Mother Ganga has found my home again!'

He got up to fill the buckets. 'Welcome, Mother. May our buckets always be filled with your blessings!'

Dada avoided the advances of the scowling neighbourhood 'water guy' and tried to keep his buckets full, though his neighbour, Chimanbhai, bought water from him occasionally when he had guests over.

As he moved back to his laptop again, Mansukhbhai Shah

wondered how he would reveal his story to his daughter-in-law and grandson that evening. It was all about peering into that line of Shahs in the past and joining the dots with his bloodline. His forehead creased and furrowed as he trawled his way through Facebook. As his involvement grew, the end of his moustache disappeared into his mouth. He was deep in his quest.

2

AN IMPOSSIBLE CHALLENGE

Chintu's day at school was not a happy one.

The classes had been okay. He had done his homework and copied his notes alright. He had narrowly missed sitting on his glasses and cracking them. So far so good.

However, the bad part was that Arjun was absent. This was an unexpected blow. Arjun was his best friend, defender and confidante. He buffered Chintu against the Gang, and in return Chintu shared his homework with Arjun whenever he needed it.

The secret horror of Chintu's life was that he stammered whenever he was very nervous. And that seemed to happen whenever the Sholay Gang approached him. He dreaded their bullying ways and avoided them as far as possible. But by late afternoon, the Sholay Gang had cornered him. His stomach dropped out of his body and left a hollow space as the Gang closed in.

'Hey Four-eyes, what did your d . . . d . . . daddy send you from D . . . D . . . Dubai?' mocked Gopal Bagadia, the King of the Gang.

'A stuffed t . . . toy for his dear b . . . boy!' echoed Rakesh, his wingman.

They hooted with laughter. The others in the class turned to watch.

'Yeah and where's your best friend today? Bunking school?' Bagadia put his hands on his hips and stuck out his chest.

The curious thing was that Chintu only stammered when the Sholay Gang teased him, or when he was nervous. All day, every day, Chintan Shah was calm and articulate. He could joke, debate and even read fluently from a book, but whenever someone from the Gang cornered him, his tongue felt like it was stuck to the roof of his mouth. And when it came unstuck, it twanged like it was tied to two rubber bands pulling in opposite directions. Twang, twang.

'Enough of all this chatter,' said Bagadia, the King, taking charge. 'Now I want some action. Gang, what say we give him a real test and see what he's made of?'

'Yeah!' Rakesh hissed. 'Give him something hard to do and shake up the scared little mouse!'

Bagadia came up close to Chintu.

'Ever seen a real tiger, Chintan Shah?' Chintu looked away.

'I . . . I . . . in the z . . . z . . . zoo.'

There was another shout of laughter as a few others in the class joined in. Bagadia's face was now six inches from Chintu's.

'Only in the zoo, huh? Well, I'll show you a wild tiger in school.'

Chintu looked away. He dared not test his tongue again.

There was an eerie silence in the classroom.

'By the end of three days, I want the pouch that hangs around Melon Man's neck.'

There was complete silence all around. This was a tough one. Melon Man was Anand Sir, the PE teacher. He was slim and well formed and his biceps bulged from his sleeves. A little green pouch hung round his neck. He never took it off and it hung around his neck as safe as a million dollar necklace.

Bagadia's voice was low and threatening.

'Did you hear? By Thursday morning, I want it here.' He pointed to the palm of his hand. 'I want to see what treasure Melon Man carries around day and night,' he said staring straight into Chintu's eyes.

'And if you don't, I'll crush your mouse tail and grind the bones out of you. You will see how Gopal Bagadia turns into a wild tiger.' Then he spun round and walked away. The Gang followed.

Bagadia chuckled to his followers. 'On Thursday, we'll see what this mouse is made of.'

The bell rang signalling the end of school.

So that was how Chintu's day passed, and there was no guarantee things would improve. In fact, the next few days promised to be worse. There was no question of getting that pouch from the well-toned PE teacher, and no point imagining what the Gang would do to him on Thursday when he failed the test. He looked out of the bus window. He would have to talk to Arjun.

★★★

At home, Dada opened the door.

'*Thepla* and milk first! You can go downstairs only after that!'

Going downstairs to play was far from Chintu's mind. He pushed away the plate of *thepla*.

'What's up, Chintya? You need to eat. No food, no mood, no good.'

Chintu silently opened his schoolbag and took out his maths book.

Mansukhbhai thought for a minute, then stood in front of Chintu. His face was serious.

Slowly, his lips widened, his fingers went to the edges of his mouth and he lifted up the corners in a smile. Suddenly, he burst into a loud cackling, chattering laugh, like a cross between a duck and a monkey.

'Oh Dada! You think I'm still five years old!' Chintu sulked.

'Arre, we are all five years old at times!' Grandfather brought out his favourite sweets and put them in front of Chintu.

'And your mood is like a puppy dog. If you want it to wag its tail and play with you, you have to make it feel good. Feed it first. Food for a good mood.'

There was a loud knocking at the door and a long whistle.

‘That must be Nandu bhaiyya!’ said Chintu and ran to open the door.

Cousin Nandu entered. Good-looking, pony-tailed, with an earring in one earlobe, a red printed T-shirt and low-waisted jeans, he sauntered in and surveyed the scene. Nandu had a demanding job with Channel 16, a TV news service. He had been working late. Returning home, he realized he had no food in his tiny rented flat and had immediately thought of Vimla Aunty, who lived down the road. There was never a shortage there. He put down his backpack.

‘So how’s our joyful family today?’ he said with a grin.

Chintu suddenly remembered King Bagadia and the challenge. He bit his lip and disappeared into the bedroom.

Nandu raised his eyebrows in a question. Mansukhbhai shrugged his shoulders. Nandu nodded wisely, winked, and followed Chintu into the room.

‘Hey Chintya, Nandu genie has a cure for all ills. Headache?’ He touched Chintu’s head. Chintu pushed his hand away.

‘Stomach hurting? Ribs aching?’ He reached out and tickled Chintu.

‘Backache? Take Dr Nandu’s pills! Neck-ache? Dr Nandu’s massage! Smile-ache? Dr Nandu’s tickles!’

Nandu’s tickling made Chintu breathless with laughter.

‘Stop! Stop! Nandu bhaiyya, stop!’

‘Give up?’

‘Okay, okay! Stop!’

Chintu had to give in to this old trick. They ended up laughing on the straw mat.

'That's better! A laugh always helps. Now tell your big brother what's going on.'

The story came out in bits and pieces as Chintu told Nandu all about the Sholay Gang, the challenge and his wayward, stuttering tongue.

'By the way, who is this Melon Man?'

'That's Anand Sir, the new PE teacher. He's nice. He's from Varanasi or something and he works out a lot and so he has big arm muscles that look like melons. That's why everyone calls him Melon Man. And no one knows what's in that pouch round his neck.'

'Ah. It must contain something special.' Things became clearer to Nandu now.

'But how come I'VE never heard you stammer?'

'It only happens when the Gang gets me. They're mean. I don't know what happens to me.'

Nandu raised his eyebrows thoughtfully.

'Do you get a hollow stomach? Go weak in the knees? Want to go to the toilet?'

Chintu was silent.

'Well, that's easy to figure out! Dr Nandu says it's fear.'

Chintu looked down.

'Listen Chintya, that's an easy-to-tackle problem if you believe you can do it! You have the power.' He brandished an imaginary sword and looked deep into Chintu's eyes.

'You are the electricity, the current that flows through. Just disconnect from the fear. Pull the plug out. Cut the connection.' He brought the invisible sword swishing down.

'What do you mean?'

Nandu sighed. 'You know the Internet and your email ID. Just quickly sign out when you feel the fear coming on. Hit the log out button and you're free. Then there's no connection. What's your service provider?'

'Gmail.'

'Okay. Imagine it's your fear. When you're scared, just sign out of it and your fear can't access you!'

'You mean I can just stop it?'

'Sure you can! Just do it. Anyway, fear isn't a service provider . . . it's a DIS-service provider! No good for you ever!'

'But how do I do it?'

Nandu paused and looked out of the small window with green shutters onto the red buses and the yellow and black cabs honking on the street below. At the corner he could see Abu Chacha cutting open the fibrous tops of his coconuts for customers. The cow lady was disappearing around a bend, leading her cow by the neck halter. He turned to Chintu.

'Breathe.'

'What?'

'It's simple. Just breathe. Slowly and deeply, for about ten seconds.'

'That's all? Breathe?'

'Yup. Ten seconds. Slow and deep.'

'And then?'

Nandu looked at him and smiled mysteriously. Then he flung out his arms.

'Then, do something dramatic, different! And quickly! Just do it.'

‘Stop joking!’ Chintu protested.

‘I’m dead serious. Lord Nandu has spoken. Trust me. Try it and tell me how it works.’ He stood up and smoothed his long black hair.

Just then Vimla entered the room. ‘Ah, Aunty’s back! Now, the table-show begins! Where’s the food?’

‘Hey Nandu, your food tank is always empty. Come on, we have enough fuel for you! Help me in the kitchen. Dada’s got something to tell us after dinner.’

As Chintu and his cousin bustled about in the kitchen, Dada arranged his chair for the post-dinner Talk.

3

THE SHADOW OF THE FUTURE

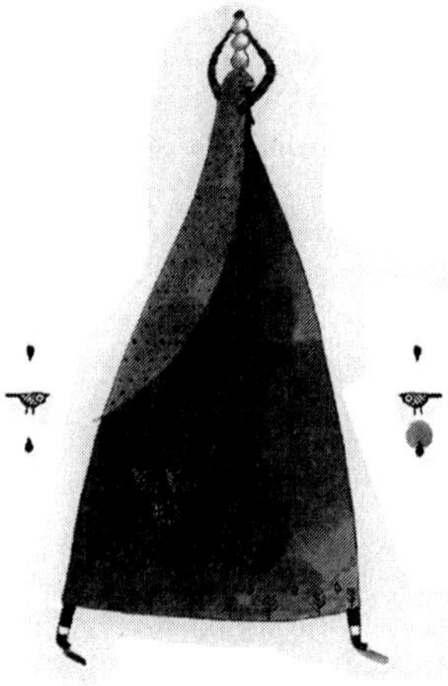

The story began 43 years ago, at 12 noon on a Saturday.

On the sunny terrace of a two-storeyed cement house in a village in his native Gujarat, a bearded man with a bright red dot on his forehead stood close to the young Mansukh. He swung him round so that Mansukh had his back to the sun.

'Stand still,' said the bearded man.

Young Mansukh obeyed. His long shadow stretched out on the terrace floor in front of him and then the bearded man did something curious. He extracted a measuring tape, a pencil and some paper. The man noted the time, and position of the sun. Then he moved around Mansukh's shadow, stalking it with his measuring tape and making notes.

Mansukh wondered how anyone could tell his future by following his shadow, taking a few measurements and marking the position of the sun. But his relatives had all gone through this and they believed in it. They had told him about this astrologer. 'In any case, what's the harm?' they said. 'It will be a bit of entertainment, if nothing else.'

Young Mansukh stood still in the sunshine. The surrounding buildings were similar to this one; two or three grey two-storeyed blocks which housed apartments, where children of all shapes and sizes ran in and out shouting and laughing loudly. On the dusty road below, cows ambled over to comfortable shady spots and a fruit-seller called out to passersby from his cart under the spreading peepul tree.

Finally, the man straightened up. He gave a brief grunt to indicate the end of the activity.

'*Chalo*. Let's go.'

They both made their way down the concrete steps, their slippers clacking on the floor.

The front room of the shadow astrologer's house was filled with a grey sweet-smelling smoke from the burning incense sticks and bundles covered in red cloth were piled in every corner. Steel utensils for his worship stood neatly together and pictures of various gods blessed them from their resting places on the walls of the room.

The man lifted a bundle of leaves to one of the pictures and tenderly unwound the cloth.

'I must inform you that these are astrological manuscripts of the ancient Brihat Samhita written in the 6th century, on leaves of the Palmyrah tree.' He paused. 'I am only a humble *Chhaaya Shastri* and I tell people's future by following their shadow, using the principles of astrology.'

A pile of neatly stacked delicate leaves emerged from the cloth. Mansukh was astonished to see words clearly etched into them.

'The art of prophesying from a person's shadow is scientific and ancient principles of astrology have been used for this. And the grace of god flows like the river to each one who invokes it.'

He touched the leaves, then pressed his fingers to his forehead. 'However, you must help.'

'What should I do, *Shastriji*?' said Mansukh as he leaned closer.

'I will read from some leaves. As I read, you must tell me if your life till now matches the prophecies I read. Only if they match your past, will I continue with that bundle of leaves. Else, a different bundle is fated for you, and I must read from that.'

'Sure *Shastriji*.'

'Now tell me, were you the youngest of three children?'

'No, *Shastriji*, I am the only child.'

The astrologer put away a bundle of leaves.

'Did you marry at the age of 23? A girl of your community, but from another village?'

'Yes, *Shastriji*. I got married last year and she was from the neighbouring village. It was a marriage arranged by my family.'

The astrologer turned several leaves as he spoke. 'Yes. Now we can proceed.'

He began reading rapidly and did not look up until the reading was done.

'You will have a happy life with one son. You will study engineering and will go on to work with the railways. Your sincerity will be rewarded. You will be promoted.'

As he read, Mansukh could picture each event as it rolled out from the leaves, through the words of the astrologer. His son, Vishnu, was not yet born, but his future was unravelling in front of his eyes as this astrologer continued to speak in a low voice. He talked about his future son's studies in pharmacy and medicine, his job, his daughter-in-law who had a job, his other relatives, his future grandson, his family fortunes . . .

'You will have a fulfilling family life but, you will never be rich.'

Mansukh felt a pang.

'Your wife will contract a disease and will be received by the gods in the seventeenth year of your marriage.'

This was an arrow through Mansukh's heart. He was just married, and very fond of his new wife.

'*Shastriji* how can this be?'

'Kindly do not disturb me in my reading. There is another thing. A person of your bloodline will be very useful to you, your family and the village you are from. There is a connection with water.'

'What does that mean?'

'Someone from your bloodline, your village and water

are all closely linked. And all will benefit each other. This is what the leaves say.'

★★★

The story-telling ended abruptly. There was silence in the living room as the listeners absorbed the story and took a while to come back to the present moment.

Mansukhbhai took off his glasses and polished them. They had all been sitting in a circle around him. The storytelling had taken half an hour.

'It all came back to me when I was cleaning up the cupboard last month and the paper with the astrologer's predictions fell out.'

'But Dada,' exclaimed Chintu, 'How can anyone tell the future from a shadow, some measurements and the sun? And how can those bundles tell the future for any person in the world?'

'Exactly what I wondered.' Dada shrugged his shoulders. 'But I don't have answers for that.'

Vimla spoke. 'Yet, he was right, wasn't he? When did Ma pass away?'

Dada winced. '17 years after we got married.' He remembered his bustling relatives discussing the illness in the hall, where the blue and purple striped carpet had been covered with white sheets. Vishnu, his son, was only fifteen then.

'And what's a bloodline?'

'Bloodline, my dear Chintya-mintya, is a descendent from the males in the family tree.'

'It's like the son of the son going way back to the earliest known male members of our family.'

Nandu stretched himself out on the narrow divan. Now I understand. 'Okay, Dada, now you need to find him.'

'Find who, Nandu?'

'The man in the village. The saviour from your bloodline. Ever since I set up the Internet connection for you, you've been on Facebook. Now I know why. You're tracing your bloodline.'

Dada shifted in his chair. 'Yes, Dr Nandu, but I still don't have a clue about the person in the prediction. I found long-lost relatives. A distant nephew happens to live just round the corner! But no one who is likely to be the "saviour" has turned up yet.'

'Your bloodline must be scattered all over the world by now. Your great grandfather's sons and their fathers before that, and their sons must have travelled to Australia, Canada, the UK, USA . . . everyone went off for better jobs.'

Vimla got up. 'Nandu's right. How would you know? And why should you search? Anyway, if it's predicted and meant to happen, it will happen anyway. Just like everything else happened. Why bother? In any case, I don't really believe in these things.'

'Maybe you're right, Vimla, but the astrologer has generally been right so far and I feel responsible somehow. It's my bloodline after all. And I'm a retired man with time to spare. I can work on it and try to connect the dots like in those newspaper puzzles. It's a quest. Most importantly . . .' he paused to make sure they were listening. 'All this will happen within THIS year . . . in the 67th year of my life . . . so let's do this now and next year we can forget all about it!'

'Coach Sahib, you might just read in the newspapers that someone from your extended family donated a lot of money for a school in your village. That'll be the end of the quest then.'

'Remember Vimla, it's not for a school. He said WATER. It's connected with water. And as you know, my village always had and still has a severe problem of water shortage.'

Mansukhbhai remembered his last visit to Tintodan ten years ago. There were queues of women in colourful attire waiting, squabbling for their share of water that arrived in a water tanker. Men climbed desperately onto the tanker which came once a week and thrust their water hoses through the lid on the top, so that water flowed into their buckets.

Mansukhbhai's family was lucky that the small ancestral house, where his cousin Chhagan lived, had a small well. Even then, the water levels were shrinking each year, and the well was almost dry in summer.

'Okay,' piped in Nandu. 'So if someone suddenly makes a donation for a few water pumps, your quest will be finished! What will you do then?'

'Ah, hmm.' Dada cleared his throat. His eyes twinkled. 'Yes. Then I will learn cooking.'

They laughed. The discussion was over.

As Chintu was falling asleep, a stray thought drifted into his head. He got up and sat by his mother who was filling out forms for a credit card. He hooked his feet up onto the chair and hugged his knees.

'Ma, do you think all this can be true?'

'Mmm, maybe. But prophecies don't always work out.'

'Ma, did Dada ever become rich?'

'He saved.'

'Then he is rich?'

'He made sure Dadi had the best treatment during her illness. That cost a lot of money.'

'But that was a long time ago.'

Vimla pushed away the forms and turned to him.

'Now, Dada won't ever tell you, so I guess I will. He spent most of the left-over money on educating your father at the best colleges in the country. He also looked after your uncle's family when your uncle moved to another town for a new job. So a lot of the money ran out,' she paused. 'But your Dada's still rich in the ways that lots of other people aren't. He's got a lot of treasure here.' She tapped Chintu on the chest. 'In his heart. And you remember that, champion!'

4

THE CONNECTION IS CUT

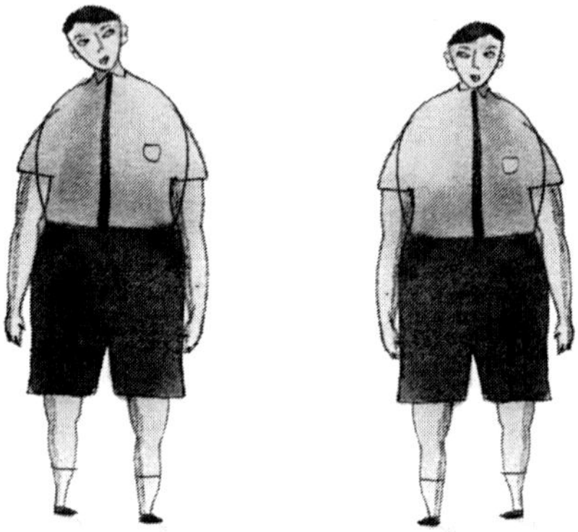

The next day, water obligingly appeared in the taps. Chintu bathed, left and waved to Abu Chacha as usual. But he was still in the world of the shadow astrologer and the strange prediction. A whole world had opened up about Dada's past and he felt that something new was about to be revealed. He felt a new connection with his larger family. After all, someone from Dada's bloodline meant that one of his relatives was soon going to be closely connected to them all through their native village. Was it really important? Probably not. But the story stayed with him nonetheless.

As soon as he reached school though, these thoughts melted away and just two things occupied all his thoughts.

1. Avoid the Sholay Gang

2. Keep Melon Man in sight

Item no 1 went down the drain immediately. Gopal Bagadia, the King, confronted him before the first period.

'So, Mr Stutter-flutter, did you get it yet? Or are you giving up?'

'Stay away, Bagadia!' Arjun came closer.

Chintu's tongue suddenly felt wobbly. He couldn't speak. His heart beat faster.

'Ha ha! Here comes your tail.'

'Stop it Bagadia,' Arjun spoke firmly.

'Your tail is trying to defend you! Does your morning milk make your tongue stick in your mouth, baby face?

'N-n-n-o.' Chintu managed. The drumming in his chest grew louder.

The King turned to his cronies.

'Did you hear that, boys? He can't utter a complete word correctly. Ha! He's such a scaredy cat.'

'Stop picking on him, Bagadia!' Arjun gripped Gopal's arm, but Gopal pushed Arjun into the corner and stepped up to Chintu.

'Scared of me, baby face?'

Two Gang members held Arjun down.

Everyone looked up to see what Chintu would do. The Gang closed in. Chintu's heart began beating like drumbeats in a rock song. Hit him? Dare not! Withdraw to his desk? Run for a teacher?

Suddenly, Nandu bhaiyya's face came back to him.

Breathe. Deeply. Slowly.

Chintu drew in his breath. One second, two seconds, three, four.

Gopal frowned suspiciously.

Then, do something dramatic, different! And quickly! Just do it.

From the corner of his eye, Chintu saw the white of the morning newspaper on the teacher's table. He pounced on the paper, spread it wide and began shouting.

'There are many reasons for water shortage. These are mainly stealing, losses within the distribution system and wasteful use. 40 per cent to 60 per cent of water is lost this way. Today, Mumbai needs over 2950 million litres of water to supply to the 21 million people who live here, and the number is growing.'

He paused to draw a deep breath.

The Gang scattered in surprise. The others began giggling. Nobody knew what had happened. Chintu could only see the black letters dancing on the white paper in front of him. His shouting grew louder, more insistent and fluent.

'The cost of water is likely to rise as new supply schemes are being planned. By 2021 the total water supply to Mumbai . . .'

Gopal got hold of Chintu's collar and yelled. 'Fool! What nonsense is this?'

The shouting was attracting attention outside the class. Miss Reena, who was on her way to the 9th grade classroom, stopped in her tracks. She had never heard Chintan Shah's voice raised this way. He had always been mild-mannered.

Miss Reena peeped in. She saw Gopal, the bully, clutching Chintan's collar and Arjun struggling in the corner. So Gopal was at it again!

But what was Chintan doing? Shouting out a news report about water problems from the newspaper? She took a quick decision. Chintan was always the quiet one in class. If he had mustered up the guts to read out the latest newspaper report about water to the class, she was going to support him.

She stepped brightly into the room.

'Not nonsense at all, Gopal. This sounds like a very interesting article on water problems in Mumbai and Chintu, by your voice I can see how concerned you are!' She paused.

'In fact, if we don't take steps now, Gopal, you might end up shovelling mud to dig a deep well!' The class tittered.

'Chintan, this is the right time for this article. The principal has just informed me about an inter-school competition on conservation and our immediate environment. Our school is taking part. We need ideas, so I'm setting up a committee for this.'

She turned to Chintu. 'Would you like to be on the water conservation committee, Chintan?'

There was complete silence in class. All eyes were on Chintu. The question sounded important. Something had clicked somewhere and somehow, Chintu had scored.

'Yes Miss Reena. Thank you.'

'Good. I'll let you know more once we are better organized.'

She walked out, her shining hair bouncing, just as the bell rang for the beginning of class.

Did she say 'conservation'? What does conservation mean anyway? thought Chintu.

Much later, in the tea break, just before Chintu ran out, Gopal strode up to him and snorted.

'Joker! Remember you have only two days left for the pouch. Then we'll see who laughs.' He turned and walked off.

Chintu had a small victory under his belt. Something strange had happened. No one quite understood how, but King Bagadia had lost without a fight. The best part was, some of the other boys had gathered round Chintu, clapped him on the back and called him a mad genius.

'What did you do? Did you go crazy or something?' asked Arjun as he plonked himself down under the tamarind tree next to Chintan during the noisy tea break.

'Arre, I don't know! It just happened! There was nothing else to do. I couldn't beat him, he would have killed me!' They opened their tiffin boxes and munched on sandwiches and *idlis*.

'Yeah. But of all things, *reading a newspaper!* Were you struck by lightning or something?'

Chintan chuckled. 'I only know I was shouting out the news as if my life depended on it!'

'Lucky that Miss Reena was passing by. She saved your life!'

'Yeah. Well I followed Nandu bhaiyya's advice.' He told Arjun all about the previous day, the breathing exercise and logging out of fear.

'Wow. Your Nandu bhaiyya sounds like a magician. Can he help you get the pouch?'

Chintan groaned. 'Oh, the pouch! I still have to get that!'

'Well now that Miss Reena's saved you, I don't think Gopal can put you in hospital if you don't get it. But we WILL get it. Now you've scored your goal, show him you can do anything. Fling the pouch in his face. Let the class laugh at him. Then you can shut his mouth forever.'

A thought struck Chintu.

'Arjun, what's "conservation"?'

'Who knows.'

Arjun stretched his legs out into the sunlight.

'I hate bullies. I have a plan. We'll get the pouch during the lunch break tomorrow.'

5

A STRANGE SCAR

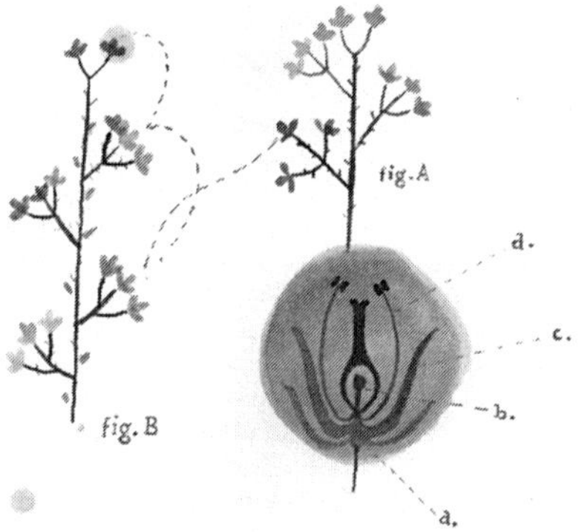

The school was built in 1951, four years after India's independence. The yellowing paint and rackety fans told their story of ageing.

In the principal's cabin, surrounded by colourful pictures, bits of children's writing and a large timetable, Principal Shashi sat alone. The familiar sounds of children's laughter at break time floated in and out of her head.

Eight months ago, her dream of heading a school had come true. Of course, she had worked hard over the years. She had taught students of all ages, participated in most school events, written research papers, advised students and teachers. She had been noticed and talked about by important officials and parents. Now, a principal at 42, she wanted to bring her school to a new level of achievement and here, in her hand, she held a letter that promised an opportunity.

She glanced again at the letter she had received three days ago from the Education Ministry.

4 May 2012

Dear Sir/Madam,

We are happy to announce that, at a meeting of the Department of Education, it was decided to organize an inter-school competition on Conservation and the Environment. Any projects that help to bring about awareness on this and related topics will be judged by eminent scholars of conservation. The judges will visit the schools on 7 June to assess the projects. The prize to the winning school will amount to three lakh rupees.

Please send in the registration for your school by 29 May 2012.

Detailed rules of the competition are attached herewith. For any questions, call 022 23870892.

Yours faithfully,
(Secretary, Ministry of Education)

Three lakhs! That was three hundred thousand rupees! She could have the entire school painted and get more laptops for the office staff! And winning would do wonders for the school's reputation!

She had already told all the teachers about the competition so they could start thinking of new projects. Her mind zeroed in on the person who could lead the project. She needed Reena Chatterjee, the biology teacher. She was enthusiastic, intelligent and able to give lots of time for school work. There was one month for preparations. Principal Shashi pictured herself receiving the prize money and smiled. Then she sighed. There was lots of work to be done before that. She pulled another bunch of waiting papers towards her.

★★★

Outside, in the compound, Anand Sir, the PE teacher, was just finishing up a class.

'Bye Sir, see you tomorrow!'

'Bye Sameer. Keep those push-ups going!'

The class had been good. He had introduced some games from his home-town, Varanasi, and the kids had liked them after the first protests. They were warming to him.

Reena was making her way to the next class. Anand's eyes lit up the moment he saw her.

'Reena*ji*, excuse me, where do we find stationery supplies? I want to do some drawings of body parts for the kids so they understand the exercises better.'

'Oh you can ask Mrs Lobo for anything you want. She's in the main office. Is everything going well?'

Anand's heart skipped a beat.

'Oh yes, thank you. I'm hoping our school will win the girls' inter-school kho-kho championship this year. I'm training the under-twelves for it.'

'Wonderful! When is it?'

'Oh it's still over two months away. Would you like to come and practice with us?'

She laughed at the question.

'Maybe I could drop by on days when classes finish early.'

'That's great! It's Mondays and Fridays after school.'

'Okay. Bye.'

Reena Chatterjee. Anand whispered her name and smiled. He had never met someone quite like her. These small daily exchanges with her brought a hint of sweetness to his life. He walked towards the men's cloak room, happily swinging his towel.

'Hi Reena, what was MM saying to you?' asked the ever-curious, slim and wide-mouthed maths teacher called Anjali or 'Miss Anju'.

'MM?'

'Arre, Melon Man. Haven't you noticed his biceps?'

'Oh is that his pet name or something?'

'That's what the kids call him. I think he likes you.'

'Hmm. Well, he's finding his way around. And he's from Varanasi. I'm sure that's pretty different from Mumbai.'

'Well, I'm just warning you, in case you hadn't noticed. Bye.'

Reena looked across the hall at Anand's receding figure. Melon Man. Yes, Anand's muscles did draw attention, but not like some superman. His yellow T-shirt hugged his torso. In fact, he was quite attractive and quite likeable. She was tuned in to the new PE teacher's presence. Her own good looks made her vulnerable, so she generally adopted an approach that took no nonsense. Back home in Kolkata, she had often glared back at young men who had stared at her. But Anand was different. There was a certain freshness about him that she liked. In fact she found it quite natural when he approached her for help in small things.

It was curious how he never spoke about that tiny green pouch around his neck, but it added to his mystery. Should she ask about it sometime? Maybe she would. The bell rang and she sprang into action.

Standard 8. Topic: Cross-pollination. She groaned. That was always an awkward one to teach.

In the cloak room, Anand splashed water over his face and looked into the mirror. Clear, brown eyes in a pleasant face looked back at him. Power-packed muscles hid beneath his yellow T-shirt.

A small smile trembled on his lips. Here was the result of hours of wrestling with the masters in the mud rings and *akhadas* back home and the constant workouts here in Mumbai, in his small flat in Andheri, which he shared with two other young men.

The smile left his face. He glanced round, reached up to the metal stopper of the main door and locked it. Then he unbuttoned his trousers, pulled them down below his hip line and lifted up his shirt. It was still there. Reflected in the mirror, to the left, below the line of his stomach, was a small, red scar.

6

THE SECRET OF THE GREEN POUCH

Dada was busy. Chintu could see this as soon as he got home. There were lists of names and there was also a blossoming family tree that was taped onto the flaking paint on the wall. He was on a full-fledged search for the descendent of his bloodline.

Chintu thought it better not to disturb him. Dada may just ask about school and he didn't want to tell him about the 'Challenge of the Green Pouch'. Chintu had to do it tomorrow under any circumstances. There was no way he could miss the deadline!

His mother came home from work and was too tired to chat much. They ate quietly and he slept early.

The next day was Wednesday. At school, Arjun whispered his plan to Chintu during the history class while Miss Telang read from the text book.

'We will do it just around the end of lunch break.'

'Are you sure it will work?'

'Of course! Leave it to me.'

Miss Telang looked up from her book and they stopped whispering.

Just before lunch, in the staff room, Anand approached Reena.

'Reena*ji*, could you show me how these marks are to be prepared?'

'Sure. It's very simple really, but just tedious work. We make nine columns for the test marks then calculate averages. I wish I knew how to use Microsoft Excel on the computer. It would make things much easier.'

'Excel? I can show you how to do it and we can work together if you like.'

'Really? Are you a computer whiz?'

'Reena*ji*, I'll tell you something. I applied to this school to teach computers, but Principal Shashi needed a PE teacher who would teach traditional sports and games. And since I had experience in those sports, she hired me for that! Actually I'm a graduate in Information Technology. Come, let's go to the computer lab and see if it's free.'

Reena's eyes widened. A whole new world of respect for Anand opened up for this attractive, modest man from Varanasi. He could go far! Information Technology professionals made a lot of money in Mumbai . . .

The computer lab was empty. They sat at a computer, their chairs close together. He explained, while she practiced on the computer. Their fingers met briefly over the keyboard. Before they knew it, their work was done. She turned to him.

'You know a lot of this stuff!'

'Well, you know a lot of biology!'

'Hmm. Do you have any more surprises up your sleeve?'

'Er, well not up my sleeve,' Anand coughed nervously.

'Well what about around your neck, then?' she teased gently and pointed to his green pouch.

Anand was startled. Was this the time to tell her? Would she understand?

'Er, um, Reena*ji*, I've been meaning to ask you something.'

'What?'

'Well, it's a little delicate.'

'Tell me.'

Anand swallowed hard.

'It's difficult to express.'

'Well, try!'

'It's about the human body.'

'Oh.'

'Certain body organs can get affected, can't they?'

'How do you mean?'

'Well, sometimes, under certain conditions, the body's organs can behave unnaturally, no?'

'Under what circumstances? I'm afraid I don't follow you Anand.'

'For example, any stimulus can make the lungs pump faster.'

'Yes, like when you run.'

'Yes or make the heart beat faster.'

Reena looked at him. What was he talking about?

'Yes that can happen.'

Anand blinked a couple of times.

'And sometimes one knows the causes for these changes and sometimes one doesn't.' Bursts of laughter floated up from the playground below.

'Forgive me, Reena*ji*, but I'm just a little nervous. You see I've never said this to anyone yet.'

Reena winced. Oh no! Her heart was beating fast . . . he wasn't going to give some kind of love speech was he?

'And I think the best way is to just say it quickly,' he went on.

'Er . . . now?'

'Yes, now.'

Anand drew in a deep breath.

'I had an operation for gall stones back home and the doctor gave me the gall stones after the operation and now I can't part with them, I don't know why, so I keep them in this pouch around my neck!'

'Oh! What? Gall stones?'

'Yes . . .'

'Gall stones around your neck? But why? Of all the things . . . gall stones?'

'Yes.'

'That's the strangest thing! But why? Gall stones are just waste stones from your gall bladder that the body is trying to throw out.

Anand was silent.

'So is that what your pouch contains? Gall stones? Waste stones from your body!'

She burst into laughter. Anand got up to go.

'No, no, wait, Anand.'

'It's okay. I didn't expect anyone to understand.'

'Oh no, it's just that . . . I didn't expect you to say that! I thought you were going to say . . .'

'What?'

'Oh never mind! I'm not laughing at you, Anand! It's just something strange and different. Sorry!'

Anand gathered his papers together. 'Well, goodbye.'

'Oh wait! It's so fascinating! Please tell me more. Why do you keep them?'

Anand hesitated.

'I really want to know. Genuinely. I didn't mean to laugh! Please tell me!'

He sat down. Without a word, he pulled the little green pouch over his head and loosened the string.

'Before the operation, they were part of my body and located deep inside it. Call me superstitious, but even though they're just waste stones from my body, I can't throw them away.'

As he spoke, he sprinkled the contents of the pouch onto the dull black mouse pad between them. Irregular pieces of translucent stone in amber, topaz and jade colours dropped out and caught the rays of the afternoon sun. They were small and delicate, almost gem-like. Reena sat silent in astonishment. Never in her life as biology student or teacher had she imagined that gall stones could be so lovely.

'Oh! Your gall stones!'

'Yes,' he said shyly. 'From deep inside me.'

They were silent as they examined the stones.

'Waste stones,' she whispered, 'and so pretty.'

'I know. They're not natural. But they're mine.'

Reena paused. The stones didn't sparkle, but caught the light and reflected subdued colours.

'Like the pearl in an oyster? Waste stone, but pretty?'

Anand relaxed and smiled. She understood.

'Exactly.'

Reena touched the stones gingerly. They felt normal. She secretly wiped her hands anyway.

'But why are you superstitious about them?'

Anand sighed. 'I don't know. It's all mixed up in my head. Your hair grows and you cut it. Your teeth fall out and that's natural. But gall stones are different. They don't happen to everyone. Inside you, they're mysteries. Once they're out, the mystery is revealed. I can't explain it.'

As they admired the stones, the thought occurred to Reena that even if no superstition was involved, Anand wouldn't throw them away. They were simply too pretty to be chucked.

The bell rang. The lunch break had begun.

7

THE CORD IS CUT

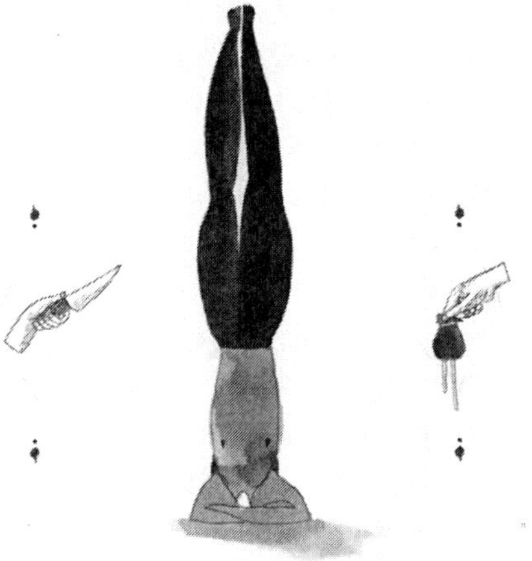

Chintu and Arjun gobbled up their lunch in 15 minutes and went looking for Anand Sir.

'I bet he's with Miss Reena. I think they like each other.'

'Let's look in the staff room first. He usually has lunch there.'

They sauntered over to the staff room and tried to peep inside as teachers came and went. He didn't seem to be inside.

'Let's go over to the canteen. Maybe he didn't have time to pack lunch.'

They saw Anand Sir emerging from the canteen.

'There he is! Let's go! Make it look casual.'

'Will it work? I don't see the pouch!' Chintu panicked.

'Relax. I can see it round his neck. Act natural.'

'Wish ourselves luck!'

'Luck? Luck comes when you wait in the bushes like a stalking tiger and the prey comes strolling by. That's what you call luck, when your chance comes and you are ready. It doesn't drop from the sky.'

'Okay, but I don't think Anand Sir's just going to stroll by us.'

'We'll stroll by and bait him. Same thing, baiting, waiting. Look. He's going down that empty corridor. Better still. Come on! Walk fast.'

They weaved their way between groups of running, shouting boys and caught up with him. 'Sir! Good afternoon Sir.'

Anand turned around. 'Hello Arjun. Hi Chintan. Have you both finished your lunch?'

'Er yes Sir. We were just wondering where you learnt all those new games . . . and how did you build your muscles?'

'Why? You want muscles too? Got a girlfriend? Want to impress her?'

'Er no, Sir . . . I hate girls. But I want to build muscles so nobody tries to hit me.'

'Hmm. Frighten your enemies away, huh? Okay. I can show you a few things.'

'Thank you, Sir. Sir, can you show me how to do *shirshaasan*? My father does yoga. He says if you can stay upside down in *shirshaasan*, your concentration improves and your arm muscles automatically improve. Can you show me?'

Anand looked quizzically at him. A yoga pose? This was a slightly odd request. Usually it was about kick-boxing or a six-pack body.'

'Ok, but you have to be very careful. Come here. Chintan and I will hold you while you try.'

'Er, ah, Sir, could YOU first show me how it's done? I'm a bit nervous and if I saw you doing it, I'd feel better.'

Anand Sir smiled indulgently. He crouched on the smooth tiles, placed his arms on the floor and smoothly swung his legs up against the supporting wall. He watched the boys with upside-down eyes. The pouch discreetly emerged and dangled temptingly near his shoulder. Arjun fingered the penknife in his pocket.

'You see it looks easy, Arjun, but needs practice.'

'Wow, Sir, how long can you stay there like that, Sir?'

'Well about four minutes.'

'Amazing, Sir! Can I watch you? Er, are you meant to keep your eyes open or shut?'

'Shut. Like this.' Anand gently closed his eyes. He began a commentary.

'You see, you must be very careful and very calm.'

In one swift, desperate movement, Arjun pulled out his penknife, flicked open the blade and delicately held the thin cord of the pouch. Then with a single stroke, he expertly sliced through it. Chintu held his breath, horrified.

'No movements. Breathe. Breathe evenly, breathe naturally,' Anand continued, eyes closed. 'And focus within, as if you are meditating.'

Arjun thrust the pouch into Chintu's hands and made frantic pushing gestures.

'GO!' he mouthed silently.

The blood drained from Chintu's face. He gasped and ran.

'The blood rushes to the head and makes the brain alert.' Anand carried on, eyes serenely closed.

'Yes, Sir, that's just what I need. Thank you so much, Sir. Er, I think I have to finish some homework before the next period. Can we practice another time? Thank you, Sir. Bye Sir!' Arjun turned and sped off.

Anand was absorbed in the yoga posture. He continued for another minute. Then he slowly rearranged his limbs downward until he was sitting upright, feeling slightly light-headed. He passed his hands over his hair, smoothing it down.

Quite refreshing, he thought, as he made his way back to the staff room. *I must do this more often. It opens up the brain's blood vessels and makes one alert. Completely alert.*

8

PLANTING STONES

Life was like a giant elastic band.

Sometimes you could do a hundred small things and bunch them all together to wrap around the day, but often, things just slipped out and had to be put into the next day's schedule which stretched and stretched worse than a big stick of chewing gum.

Principal Shashi was beginning to experience this. There were just too many things to do. She suddenly pushed aside her papers. Something had to be planned for the contest first. What could her school do with the resources they already had? Conservation. Water. Plants. Vegetables. Food. *Food.*

Principal Shashi's deprived stomach began growling. She glanced at her watch. Ah, it was still lunchtime. Conservation could wait for the moment. Her feet obeyed the call of her tummy and took her towards the school's cafeteria.

Chintu was worried. He had grabbed the pouch and run. But now, Anand Sir's pouch felt like a hot potato burning up his pocket. What to do with it? Where to hide it? Chintu dared not take it to class. What if Anand Sir discovered the loss and had him searched? He could clearly visualize the scene.

'I suspect someone has been stealing my property. Arjun and Chintan stand up! Turn out your pockets. There's my pouch! Thieves! Call your parents immediately! I'll have you rusticated! I'll . . .'

No, can't risk all that. I need to find a hiding place quick and come back for it later, thought Chintu

He thrust the pouch deep into his pocket and walked quickly towards the kitchen. The kitchen wall was located next to the school compound wall which adjoined the main road. On the other side was the cafeteria. There was a long, narrow strip of land between the kitchen and the inner wall, where the cooks threw the vegetable peels, the unwashed veggies and the general kitchen garbage. This was the section the school authorities generally avoided, since the smell of rotting food hung here like a cloud. Chintu picked up a grubby stick and poked at the soil near the tank. The corner of the tank would do, and he could cover the pouch with some soil. He pulled the pouch out of his pocket.

'Chintan Shah, what are you doing here?'

Chintan's heart almost shot out of his body. He rocketed around and stared into Principal Shashi's cucumber-green eyes. His nerves began twanging like a broken sitar string.

'Oh, er, er, Ma'am, I was just, er . . . just . . .'

'Is that a stick in your hand?'

'Er yes, er . . . I . . . I am d . . . d . . . digging.'

'Digging? Digging in this pile of vegetable peels?'

'Er . . . no Ma'am. Er y . . . yes Ma'am . . . I was j . . . just . . .'

'Now don't try to fool me. You've got a secret here, haven't you?'

'Er no, Ma'am, I w . . . was j . . . just er, you s . . . see . . .'

'Miss Reena has been telling me about your interest in conservation. Is it something to do with that?'

'Well, no, er y . . . yes . . . I mean . . .'

'What's that in your hand?' She jerked the pouch out of his hand.

Chintu wished he were on another planet, another time zone, a cartoon character in the newspaper . . . anything but real and right there, right now.

'Ooh! What are these?' she was turning the small stones over in her hand. 'Never seen anything like these!'

'Well, it's s . . . s . . . special, Ma'am. You see, Ma'am, you s . . . s . . . see . . .'

'See? See? Seeds! Ohhh! I'm beginning to understand now! These are seeds. Isn't that what you were trying to say? And you're going to plant these and use the vegetable peels as compost! How brilliant!'

Breathe! Breathe! Thank you Lord Shiva, Ganesha ji, Saraswati ji, Lakshmi ji!

'Y . . . y . . . yes Ma'am. Are . . . are . . .'

'Are? Are? Oh yes, the 3 'R's! Reduce! Re-use! Recycle! Re-use the peelings, reduce waste! Use this waste strip of land to plant a vegetable patch with these seeds! Create more food!'

Saved, saved! Thank you all gods! Breathe, breathe! Deeply and evenly.

'Oh yes, Ma'am. Vegetable patch. Seeds. Con . . . conser . . . conserVATION!' He struggled with the last word which emerged like a bullet.

'Well, I'm proud of you, Chintan Shah. What seeds are these?'

The drum beat began again. 'Er . . . er . . . s . . . special. D . . . d . . . donno.'

'That's no problem.' She slipped the seeds into the pouch. 'Miss Reena should know. She's the biology teacher. We'll find out from her. We can organize the compost and begin working on the vegetable patch immediately. In a week, plants will peep out. When the award committee comes, we will have . . .' she stopped her happy train of thoughts and turned to Chintu, dangling the pouch.

'You can return to class, my dear. I'll take care of it now.' She beamed and walked off, her head teeming with new ideas.

Chintu sat down heavily on the rusty tank, his head buried in his hands. Talk about roller coaster rides . . . this one had almost made his insides fall out! And . . . he had just lost the hard-won pouch!

In the distance, just outside the staff room, Miss Reena met Principal Shashi.

'Oh Reena, here are some seeds. I found fifth grader Chintan Shah trying to plant them. I think he has some ideas about our conservation competition and composting with the waste from our kitchen. Could you have a look and see which seeds these are? Quite pretty, I thought.'

The all-too familiar pouch hung between her thumb and index finger.

Reena's eyes widened in puzzlement.

Anand's pouch! How . . . who . . . ?

'I'd be grateful if you could encourage the boy,' Principal Shashi continued. 'He stammered his way through the explanation. I had to guess the whole story, he was hesitating so much! Do you think you could give his project an extra ten points?'

Reena collected herself.

'Sure, I'll do what I can. I'll take these . . . er . . . seeds and have a look.' She grasped the pouch, smiled sweetly and walked off.

This was Anand's pouch for sure! Chintan Shah . . . again! Hmm. He would never try pinching Anand's pouch for fun. No, he must have been forced to do this. Maybe Gopal had something to do with it. Gopal the bully . . . she remembered the scene with Gopal Bagadia.

'Reena*ji*!' Anand's face had lost its colour.

'Anand, what's the matter?'

'My gall stones! The pouch is gone!'

Reena couldn't miss this chance to tease him.

'How?'

'Well right after I showed some fifth graders how to do *shirshaasan*, I realized that the pouch had gone. Perhaps the cord was worn out and the pouch fell off. I can't find it anywhere!' he panted with anxiety.'

'Why not ask Principal Shashi if she's seen it?'

'I can't do that!'

'Why not?'

'Can you imagine me asking her if she'd seen a pouch full of my gall stones? She'd think I'd gone kooky!'

Reena laughed inwardly as the jigsaw puzzle was slowly coming together in her mind. 'By the way, who were these fifth graders?'

'Oh, Chintan Shah and Arjun.'

Chintan again, shirshaasan, *cord worn out, seeds . . . she almost had the whole picture now.*

'Leave it to me. If you are destined to keep the gall stones, they will come and I will see that they are in your hands tomorrow before lunchtime. If not, then they were meant to part from you.' She touched his arm lightly, gave a reassuring smile and sauntered off, curls bouncing.

Anand watched puzzled as well as touched by her concern. His arm was both fire and ice where she had touched it.

9

THE HIDDEN PROPHECY

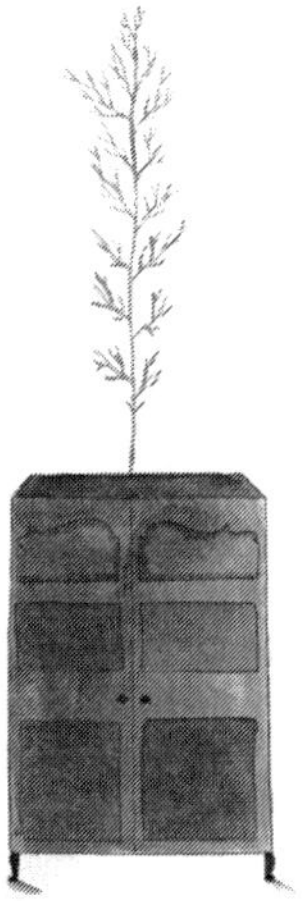

Mansukhbhai was delighted. He was decorating his bedroom wall by himself with streams of paper and Chintu's colour pencils. Blue names for all the family on his eldest uncle's side, red for the youngest uncle's family and yellow, green and black for relatives from his grandfather's generation. He was tracing back his bloodline and discovering people who had previously been shadows of the past and were now suddenly coming alive! And imagine discovering all of this in his 67th year!

What a discovery Facebook was! What did Nandu call it? Social networking! Yes, it was wonderful! And now there was Twitter as well!

Besides, the flaking paint on the wall was all covered over and hidden by the strips of papers. The room definitely looked more cheerful.

He swung the folds of his *dhoti* out of the way and sat cross-legged on his bed. Yet, he was not any closer to zeroing in on the 'saviour'. Most of his extended family had left the village for a better education, better jobs, a better lifestyle and were now scattered in India and abroad, just as Nandu had guessed. He had no phone numbers beyond that of his cousin, Chhagan, and he couldn't discuss the prediction with him. It sounded too vague, and Chhagan might think he was going soft in the head. He needed to go there himself. Soon.

A sudden twinge of pain clouded his face. He doubled up on the bed and waited till the spasm left him. In a couple of minutes, he carefully straightened up again.

He opened the worn wooden cupboard and took out the old papers once more. He had written the predictions in his slanting looped handwriting, trying to keep to the actual words of the *Chhaaya Shastri*.

In your 67th year, someone from your bloodline will benefit your village. The benefit will be connected with water in some way. ***That may also be the last year of your life.***

Grandfather stood up and looked out of the window. The street below was teeming with noisy cars and people as usual.

That may also be the last year of your life.

The words echoed in his head. Of course he had left out that part when he was telling the story to the three listeners the other day. He wasn't going to let anyone worry about it. Besides, he already knew he was getting close to the finish line. His doctor friend had already told him he had Haine's Disease, which was a critical illness, and Mansukhbhai had made him swear not to tell the others.

Oh well, life had been good. This old, greying calendar had enjoyed some happy, red-letter days! He'd had a loving wife, a hard-working son, a caring daughter-in-law and a well-brought-up grandson. Whatever was left of life was a bonus and he was going to enjoy every minute right till the end. He walked to the kitchen. Chintu would be home soon.

10

DEB AND LI

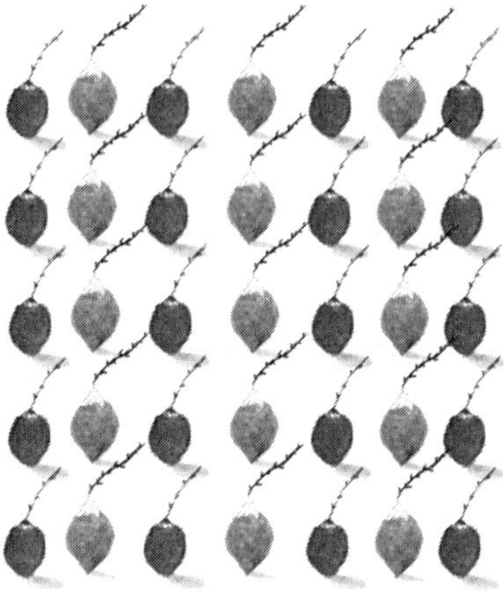

The school bus drew up at the corner. Chintu wobbled out and stood for a moment, clutching his schoolbag, pale and quiet.

Bad day, thought Abu Chacha as he looked at Chintu.

'Hey Chintu baba, I've just cut open an extra coconut. Here, drink up! It's the drink of the gods!' he gestured to the wooden box in his stall and held out a coconut.

'No thanks Abu Chacha.'

'Oh come on now; never refuse a good, healthy offer! Here's a straw.'

Chintu sat down and took the coconut.

'Bad day, huh? Sometimes I have bad days too! Yesterday some well-dressed man in a car ordered six coconuts for everyone in his car and haggled and haggled over them as if that was the last wish of his life and it was my job to fulfil it!

'So what did you do?'

Chacha chuckled. 'I told him to try drinking tea instead!'

Chintu pictured Abu Chacha, surrounded by his coconuts, telling the man to drink tea, while all his car-mates watched. He giggled. Then he remembered his own crazy roller-coaster day.

'Chacha, what do you do when you're in trouble and you can't do anything about it?'

'Real trouble?'

'Real bad trouble.'

Abu Chacha wiped his long sharp knife on his *lungi*.

'I pray. I pray to Allah and then leave it all to him. He's my closest friend.'

'Does he listen?'

'Sure.'

'And then he makes everything alright?'

Abu Chacha tapped a coconut to check its ripeness.

'He makes everything the way it needs to be. He tells me to follow DEB & LI.'

'DEB & LI? Who on earth are they?'

'Well,' he said as he took some empty coconuts and stacked them up in the corner. 'He always wants the best for me. And my best and his best may not match. I may want hundreds of thousands of rupees, but that may not be the best for me.'

'Why not?'

Abu Chacha put his hands on his hips. 'Because then I would be living in a big house, driving a big car and ordering people about and not be a good coconut seller, having these nice little chats with you!'

Chintu thought about it.

'So do you just let Allah do everything for you?'

Abu Chacha laughed.

'I pray to Him but I don't expect Him to buy my coconuts, to keep my accounts, to sell my used coconuts to the scrap merchant. That's my job. The Lord helps you if you make an effort to help yourself. You have to do your work properly, and only after that, leave everything to the Lord. In your case, Chintu, you go to school, so you must study well!'

Chintu sucked thoughtfully at the straw. 'So who or what's DEB & LI?'

'Do Everything Best & Leave It. DEB & LI.'

'Leave It?'

'Yes. You have to try to do everything as best you can, and then leave it. Let the Lord decide what should happen after that. Simple.'

Chintu dripped the last of the sweet water into his mouth.

'Thanks Chacha. I'll remember that.'

'Okay son, run home now. Your Dada will be waiting.'

11

MISS REENA TO THE RESCUE

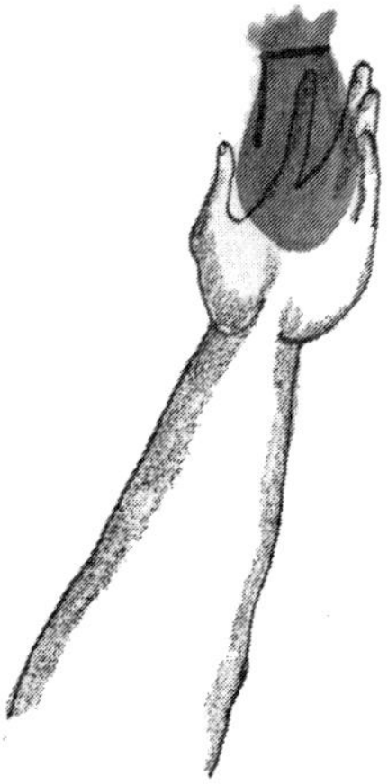

By Thursday morning, after much arguing with Arjun over the phone, Chintu decided to go and confess everything to Principal Shashi; Gopal Bagadia, the challenge, the pouch and tricking Anand Sir. After all, it wasn't his fault. It was a challenge, and even though he was bullied into it, the only self-respecting thing to do was to accept it. It wasn't such a big crime and she would not chuck him out of school for it.

He entered school and was accosted by Miss Reena. Without a word, she held up the pouch. The drumming in his chest began again.

'Did you take this from Anand Sir?'

'Y . . . y . . . yes Miss.' He was not going to mention Arjun's part, if he could help it.

'Why?'

He looked at Miss Reena. She looked steadily back at him. He could trust her. He leaned against the wall, took a breath and in a few minutes, he poured out the story; the challenge, the newspaper, *shirshaasan*, cutting the cord, the kitchen, Principal Shashi and the loss of the pouch.

Miss Reena listened without saying a word.

'What exactly did Gopal say?' she asked.

'He said he wanted the pouch in his hand in three days. That's today, Thursday.' Chintu said miserably.

Miss Reena chuckled.

'In his hand, hmm? Alright, Chintan, you and I are going to have a little deal. I will take care of the challenge right now. And in return, you have to be the leading man on my water committee. Deal?'

'Yes, Miss Reena, but how?'

'Don't worry, just leave it to me. Come on. Let's go to class.'

'Miss . . . er what are those seeds?'

Reena was silent for a few seconds.

'Stones. Precious stones. But Shashi Ma'am thinks they're seeds. Don't worry, I have some useful seeds we can use as substitutes.'

Precious stones! No wonder he carried them around his neck. Wonder how much they were worth. Before he could say anything, he was being propelled to his classroom where the rest of his classmates were milling around waiting for the morning bell to ring. Arjun looked up surprised to see Chintu with Miss Reena. What was up?

'Good morning everyone.' Miss Reena's voice was chirpy. The noise died down and everyone looked at her.

She walked up to Gopal.

'Gopal, did you ask Chintan to do something for you? Something that he had to do by today?'

Gopal was shocked. Had that dumb Chintan complained to the teachers about him? Weasel! He would have him by the neck at break time.

'Er . . . no . . . er . . . yes Ma'am.'

'Good. Well, he didn't want to tell me, but I found out, and I thought I might help you both in this task.

'M . . . m . . . Ma'am?'

'I've got what you wanted. In return, will you agree to do something for us? Is it a deal?'

'N . . . no, Ma'am . . . I mean, y . . . y . . . yes, Ma'am . . .'

'Good.' She dangled the pouch in front of Gopal's eyes. The class gasped. 'Is this what you wanted?'

'No . . . er . . . Ma'am, I . . . I mean y . . . y . . . yes, Ma'am.'

Strangely, Gopal was stammering and beginning to sound a bit like Chintu.

'I understand you wanted it in your hand. Hold out your hand.'

Gopal gingerly held out his hand, expecting a blow. Instead, Miss Reena placed the pouch gently on his palm and let it rest there for a couple of seconds. Then she whisked it away.

'There. You had it in your hand. The task is done. Are you satisfied?'

'But Ma'am . . . er . . . no Ma'am. I mean er, Y . . . yes, Ma'am.'

'Good. Now, for your part of the deal. Congratulations, Gopal, I'm making you the head of the cleaning committee. So your first job is to dig and clean out the waste behind the kitchen. We are using that area for a kitchen garden to plant vegetables for us and the kitchen waste will be used for composting. You can start from tomorrow. Miss Lobo will give you a strong broom and waste bucket.'

There was general laughter. She turned to the class. 'Is that a fair deal in return for Chintan's task?'

'Yes Ma'am!' The class, suppressed for long by Gopal's bullying ways, shouted their approval. Satisfied, Miss Reena shook her curls and strode off.

The class gathered round Chintu and clapped him on the back.

'You hit a sixer!'

'Yeah, it was a golden goal!'

'Bagadia's new name—"Dig dig Digadia"!'

He countered question after question about his new feat. Meanwhile, Gopal Bagadia was left in a corner of the classroom, the Gang slinking away quietly from him.

Miss Reena ran up to Anand just as the bell rang.

'Fate was kind. Here it is, intact.' She held out the pouch, now rather grubby from handling. 'And I suggest you keep the stones in a quiet place at home. They've been through too much excitement already.' She gave him a mischievous smile, turned and strode off to her first class for the day leaving a dumbstruck Anand behind.

12

THE GREAT CONSERVATION PROJECT

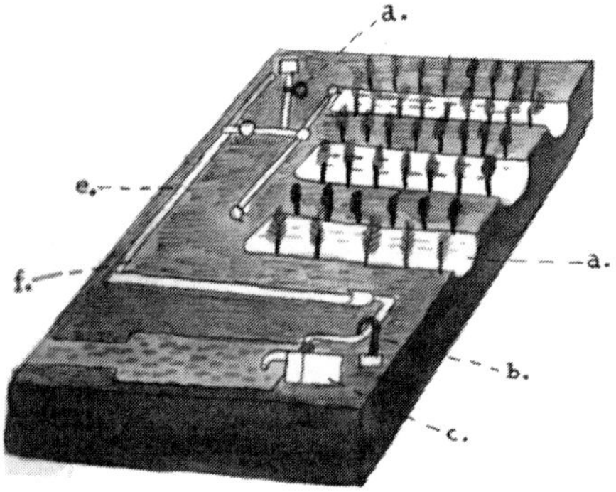

Ever since the letter from the State Government had come, Principal Shashi had become a Lady with a Mission. Their school must win. WOULD win. Her teachers shared the project ideas suggested by the students. Deadlines were set for teachers and students of each class.

'We might as well live in school,' complained Shrikant, who had been spending time both before and after school hours on his project. 'I am such a fool! I gave the idea for a newspaper collection competition and they made me team leader! Now I have to run to every class after school and remind them to bring newspapers the next morning!'

Every day, old newspapers piled up in each class. At the end of the week, he would measure the height of each pile to decide which class had won. Then most of the newspapers would be sold to the local scrap merchant. The money was used buy art materials, and the rest given to the art teacher to be recycled for papier mache items for the students' art project.

'And I have to help that bully Bagadia dig that filthy dump next to the kitchen. It's going to be a compost heap to grow veggies,' Alim added.

Just then Principal Shashi strode in. 'Well, once we have our vegetables growing in that useful strip of land, we may be able to provide organically grown food AND reduce our lunch costs! Wouldn't that make your parents happy!' She smiled.

'And by the way, I have a piece of news that will interest all of you.'

Some drama was needed. She had worked hard to achieve this feat and was now ready to drop the bombshell.

'All the students of the winning school will get to meet Aamir Khan. He will personally hand out the certificates to deserving candidates.'

There was a collective gasp in the room.

'I've just been telling the other classes. So I hope that by the time we return from our mid-term break in three weeks, we can exhibit all the wonderful things we have been doing! Have a good day children.' Smiling at their star-struck faces, she turned and left.

'Aamir Khan!'

'So what? Who cares? We shake hands and get a certificate in three seconds. I'm sure that makes no difference to him anyway,' Hardik grumbled. 'We break our backs to do all this stuff. For him it's one hour of smiling while everyone else goes cross-eyed staring at him. And then he gets to be in all the newspapers, while we are the ones doing the hard work.'

Ketan spoke up. 'Oh stop whining! We'll be in the papers with him.'

There was a pause.

'Yeah.' said Arjun. 'Anyway, he's so COOL!'

That summed up the situation.

And so, quite quickly, the contest got under way. As the days passed, the school's interest in conservation escalated. Like a stone dislodged from the top of the hill, the focus on conservation began rolling and gathering speed. It all actually became interesting.

Miss Telang, the history teacher, planned a trip to Ahmedabad to see how wise kings of the past ordered the building of Adalaj ni Vav, an ancient step well. Medicinal herbs were planted around it. These herbs fed their healing powers into the waters, so people could drink it and stay healthy.

In the EVS class they decided which plants would be best suited for the kitchen garden patch, using the waste water left over from cooking.

The science teacher organized a trip to visit Chhatrapati Shivaji's forts to see how water streams hidden in rocks were tapped and used for daily needs. The water from these streams was guided into the dark, natural caves inside the fort, to keep the water from evaporating in hot weather. Another group worked on something called 'drip irrigation', which was really as simple as taking pipes with holes in them and laying them along the ground. The holes in the pipes dripped water straight into the soil. That way, the water didn't evaporate and get wasted. 'More crop per drop', they called it.

Other classes were doing projects too. The eighth graders were working on ways to save electricity. The ninth graders were going out after school and visiting people to do a survey of how much garbage families produced and what they did with it. They were making a map of the area around the school.

'Listen, boys, this is all very well. You do your projects, we enter the competition, we win the prize and shake hands with Aamir Khan. All that's great!' Miss Anju was in charge today.

'But what does it do for you every day? When you finish school and go home? Does it all fly out of the window?'

Chintu imagined his green metal windows with the thin flowered curtain fluttering against it and all his school work flying out through them along with the compost pit. It was an exciting thought.

Instantly, Arun's hand shot up. 'Ma'am, I save electricity! I do my homework by the light of the TV!'

There was a shout of laughter from the room.

'Arun, you'd better switch off the TV and save your eyes and your brain too!' This was greeted by more laughter

'You need proper light for reading. You have to decide when you need energy and when you don't.'

Chintu pictured his own home. Grandfather's small room had a tube light and the other room where his mother and he slept, had another tube light. One yellow light shone above the dining table outside. All these lights were needed.

Chintu's mind wandered off.

It was the heart of summer. These days, the sun filled the classroom with heat. Chintu remembered how, in the monsoons, the gusts of wind shook the bags of rain out of the clouds and let them loose on the world.

'Water is going to be scarce. They say the next war will be fought for water,' Miss Anju's words hung in the hot air.

'Can't we sell some of our rain? We get a lot in the monsoons,' asked Chintu.

Bagadia guffawed. 'Selling rain? What a fool!'

Miss Anju ignored Bagadia. 'That's an idea! When we have more than enough of something, we sell it or export it to another place that needs it.

'You mean we can really export our water?'

'Well, in India itself, some states share river water with other states and pay their share. They pay for the water they get from other states.'

This was a new and weird thought. Chintu always thought water was free. It's true it didn't always stream out of the tap when he wanted it, but how could you buy or sell it like toothpaste or a bar of soap?

Dada hadn't told him about the scowling man and others like him who stole water and sold it at high prices.

'And in the future, if water is going to be scarce, we need to conserve it. Here's a list of things that you can do to save water. Take a sheet, check if you are doing any of these things already, then take the sheet home and see how you can start making changes at once.'

Chintu collected his sheet and studied it.

WATER SAVING AT HOME! DO YOU FOLLOW THESE TIPS?

1. Turn off the taps when brushing teeth?
2. Put a full load of clothes into the washing machine?
3. Shower for only seven minutes at the most?
4. Wash dishes without the tap running at full throttle?
5. Wash fruits and vegetables in a pan instead of running water from the tap?

Hmmmm. As Chintu went through the list, he began to wonder. He didn't have a washing machine and he always had a bucket bath since the water usually came only after he left for school.

'Who's the head of the water committee? Ah, Chintan. Tell me, do you follow any of these tips?'

As Chintu looked through his list, an important realization was creeping up on him. Conserving water meant saving it! You could save it in so many ways.

He thought about his everyday life. All those hours of waiting for the water to emerge from the taps, the quick filling up of the green plastic buckets in the bathroom, the vessels piled up in the kitchen sink, his mother's chatter while washing the vessels . . . all this was his normal routine, and IT WAS ALL ABOUT USING LESS WATER! IT WAS ABOUT CONSERVATION! Nobody told him that he and his family had been practicing conservation all this time! He was sure all those years in the past had taught him 'conservation' just so that he could enjoy this moment of triumph . . . it was all meant for him, for this question and this moment in class.

'Well?'

He took a deep breath.

'Oh yes, Ma'am. We do all these things. And some more!' he looked up, eyes shining.

Miss Anju raised her eyebrows.

'Alright then, tell us.'

Home. The bathroom. The kitchen. No running water. Chintu pulled out of his memory the pictures of his mother and grandfather doing the water balancing act.

'Er, I always have a bucket bath, no shower. That needs less water.'

No washing machine. 'My mother soaks the clothes first, then she washes them by hand.'

Ma is tired at night. 'And she soaks the pots and pans after dinner, so she needs less water to scrape them clean at night. We even have different water glasses, so we drink as much as we want and cover the glass instead of throwing away the remaining water.'

The green pot on the window sill. 'Then at night we pour the remainder into our plant.'

He had never spoken so much in class before.

'And I also pour the extra water from my water bottle into the school plants at the end of the school day.' *Why carry the extra weight back home!*

Miss Anju was more than surprised. This quiet boy was turning out to be quite a gem.

'Well, Chintan, you should be elected to the government's Municipal Water Works! Can you tell us how you learned to do all this?'

'I learnt it because I had to do it! We get water for just

four hours a day. So we HAVE to save water!' he declared triumphantly.

Any second now, the class would break into clapping for those years that Chintu had been conserving water, saving it, doing everything Miss Anju was talking about. Instead, there was a shout of laughter from the back of the class where Bagadia sat.

'Only four hours of water! Poor baby face!'

'Go eat chillies, Bagadia.' It wasn't Arjun. It was Ketan. His voice was low and threatening. Chintan looked round in surprise. He didn't know he had more friends here.

Miss Anju moved swiftly.

'Yes, Gopal Bagadia, don't you have water cuts at home?'

Gopal sniggered. 'No, Ma'am.'

'Oh well, too bad. We ALL ought to have water cuts, to understand how important water is. Chintan seems to be the only lucky boy around!'

Everyone looked at Bagadia and laughed.

'So, all of you take these sheets of paper to your family and tell me how you are saving water. Friday is when we meet again for discussions. Well done, Chintan.'

He was the star again. Ketan and a group of new friends surrounded Chintan. His chest felt like it had a bag full of happiness stuffed inside it. On the way home, he waved to Abu Chacha, sprinted along his street, up the stairs, and buried his finger in the doorbell button till the door shot open.

'Tsunami? Fire? Earthquake?' Dada wiggled his eyebrows up and down, making big eyes behind his glasses.

'Dada, I'm the head of the water committee! We are going to win the prize. Three lakhs. And Aamir Khan's going to shake our hands!' All the latest news cartwheeled out of him as he gobbled up his *thepla.*

'Yes, we are the no 1 water conservation family simply because we get so little water! The government will give us a medal even if your school doesn't win.' Dada picked up Chintu's empty glass and walked to the kitchen.

Chintu paused a moment. It was true he saved water. But he longed to have a hot bath sometimes when the days were cooler. A long, hot *shower.*

'Now wash your mouth and go on downstairs to play. Come up by 6 p.m. and then you can tell me more.'

But the worst of the roller-coaster rides was to come in the next few minutes.

As Chintu swung the front door open to go downstairs, he heard a chair hit the ground behind him. He turned to find Dada writhing in pain on the floor and the empty glass of milk shattered in pieces around him.

The moments that followed were hurried and blurred. Chimanbhai came, followed by the other neighbours. The glass was swept up, telephone calls were made, Dada was placed on his bed to recover and Ma appeared.

Unfamiliar voices and sounds filled their small flat as the light outside the window changed from yellow to grey. Finally, night set in as the doctor left, the neighbours and friends filtered out and Chintu was left with his mother.

Vimla sighed. 'Thank goodness. Doctor Uncle says it's a bit of weakness. He said Dada needs vitamins and an iron injection. He'll come and give it tomorrow.'

'But he was clutching his stomach.'

'Yes, Dada says he hurt himself on the chair as he fell. Now go to sleep. He'll be better tomorrow after his vitamins.'

Chintu said nothing. Dada had fallen BEFORE the chair upturned. Vimla moved over to him and hugged him tightly. 'Sleep will do us all a lot of good, including Dada. Everything will be back to normal tomorrow.'

Chintu got off his bed and parted the curtain at the entrance to Dada's room. The light was on but Dada was snoring. Chintu bent over him. Dada's face was calm, moustache slightly skewed, hair tousled. Something was poking out from under his pillow. It looked like some yellowed sheets of paper. Chintu pulled them out from under his grandfather's head and glanced at them.

'. . . 67th year, someone from your bloodline . . .'

67th year? Ah . . . the predictions.

Chintan stacked them neatly and began folding them. Suddenly, something caught his eye.

'. . . last year of your life.'

Last year of your life. What was that? Chintu unfolded the paper again and read.

'In your 67th year, someone from your bloodline will benefit your village. The benefit will be connected with water in some way. That may also be the last year of your life.'

Through the mist of the confused events of the evening, Chintu began to understand. Dada's walls covered with diagrams of the family tree and the urgency of the quest. He was 67 now! If the earlier predictions were true, then this prediction . . .

'That may also be the last year of your life.'

Chintu could hear the familiar drumbeat begin again in his chest. He folded the papers and replaced them. *The last year of Dada's life?* He stood for a moment and breathed deeply for ten seconds. Then he crept silently into bed and covered himself with the sheets.

No. Everything would not be back to normal tomorrow. Nothing would ever be normal again.

13

GOING AWAY

Somewhere, a stopwatch was ticking. It ticked incessantly, through Chintu's waking hours and sleeping hours. It ticked away in the background during his classes. It was loudest when Chintu was by himself. It didn't have anything to do with the contest because that was going full steam. No, it was different. A lifeline was ticking, a bloodline was ticking and the stopwatch was in his heart. He had to do something for Dada.

Suddenly, Chintu realized he was a helpless eleven-year-old and a grown-up at the same time. With his father in

Dubai, he was the man of the house. He couldn't tell his mother about Dada. She might break down. He couldn't tell his father as he had no more leave and might lose his job if he returned to Mumbai before his contract finished. Dada refused to visit Doctor Uncle again and Doctor Uncle said he just needed vitamins. Chintu had confided only in Nandu bhaiyya, who had come visiting every day after that. He had to be strong. What could he do for Dada? More than ever, he had to find the saviour from his bloodline. That's what Dada spent all his days on and wanted above everything.

Each day, he took longer to eat his *thepla* after school as he chatted with Dada and watched him carefully.

And then there was school. The stopwatch ticked in time with his heartbeats.

School now resembled a factory. Principal Shashi had pulled out all the stops. For the next weeks, whatever topics had to be studied in class were somehow linked to their conservation projects. Painted papier mache flower vases were created to be presented to grandfathers and grandmothers. Waste cartons were cut, decorated, varnished and placed around the school as waste bins. Vegetables were planted in the no-man's land outside the kitchen which had been raked with earth and segmented. Plastic cans and bottles were collected, their tops sliced off and used as containers for classroom plants. Days came and went like an endless stream.

'What are WE going to do?' The water committee debated at lunch time. Different voices were tossing about opinions.

'Look, all we need to do is to get ideas from the Internet. Lots of schools must have done work on water.'

'Yeah, then should we just copy some of them?'

There was an uneasy silence. Copying others' ideas was not heroic.

Finally, Arjun had a brainwave.

'Since everyone is trying to conserve, let's put up a huge 20-foot-long poster all along the inside of the dining hall wall. We can get everyone to write whatever they are doing in their lives, to save water! Then the whole school can be involved and it will be like a daily record right up to the time of the contest!' There was a general thumbs up for this and more ideas were generated around this.

'Two weeks and six and a half feet of newspapers. That's about 30 kilograms! We can get three hundred rupees for 30 kilos from the scrap paper merchant. Not bad for a starter!'

The 7th Standard kids were working on how LED bulbs could save 80 per cent energy compared to incandescent bulbs. The 7th Standard group was sent to study with them. They learnt from them what light means in our lives and both classes prepared a joint project.

Standard 4 was spending their Environmental Science classes with Standard 6. Behind the gym, the 4th graders placed pots and planted and labelled new plants donated by a nearby park. The 6th graders sketched the parts of these plants from the seed to the first shoots that popped up above the mud in the pots.

Two hectic weeks into the preparations and life was divided between Dada, school and homework. But Chintu couldn't make that background ticking go away. Something had to be done for Dada and he wasn't sure what. Everything seemed urgent.

Then, one evening, Fate suddenly sprung a surprise.

Mother got up from the dinner table with a letter in her hands, and approached Dada.

'Coach*ji*, there's a letter from Chhagan Kaka from Tintodan.'

'Chhagan? What does he say?'

'He's having a grand ceremony on 6 June. It's the 50th birthday of our family temple. He wants us to be there. I'll write and tell him we can't go.'

'No, wait.' The corner of Dada's moustache disappeared into his mouth. He chewed on it thoughtfully.

'I will go.'

They both looked at him.

'Yes, Coach Sahib, I suppose you will go, find your saviour there and reward him with your vitamins and your iron injections!'

'I need to go.'

'Arre but . . .'

Chintu's heart raced. He made a quick calculation.

'Mother, that's when I have a mid-term break, before the inter-school competition. We can all go together.'

'Yes,' Dada said. 'Good idea, Chinty. Let's plan.'

'Arre you two can't just climb onto your horses and start your race! Let me think.'

'What is there to think about? Take leave from the office, we pack up and go!'

'Oh, and who will get the train tickets, tell the milkman, newspaperman, cleaning lady . . .'

'No problem. I will do all that and Nandu will get us the tickets.

Mother picked up the dishes from the table.

'Well I suppose we could . . .'

'That's done then.'

But it didn't quite happen like that. Dada had another seizure while everyone was away. He recovered by himself and told no one. But after a thoughtful munch on the end of his moustache, he decided he didn't want panic and more questions on the trip. He dropped out.

'I have to oil up my old bones. Too rusty for this trip right now. Now Chintu, are you going to cry because I'm not coming?'

'Dada, I'm eleven years old now! That's five plus six!'

'Oh, oh how time flies! Alright alright, I was always bad at maths.'

He convinced Vimla and Chintu to carry on, while Nandu stayed with him. They were to leave on Friday night and be back within five or six days. They agreed to call each other every day. Chintu also promised to look out for the potential 'saviour'.

14

TRAIN TO TINTODAN

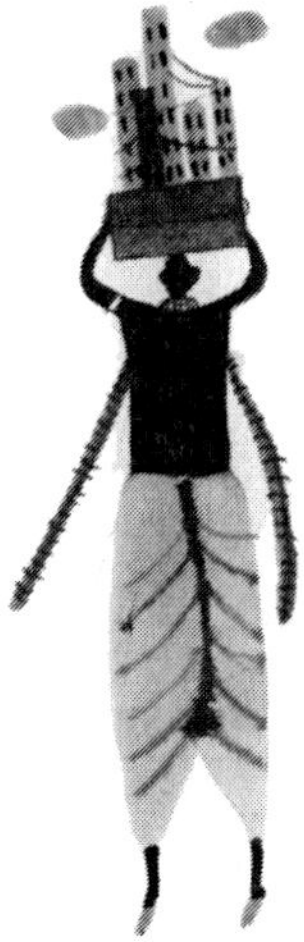

The luggage was stored under dusty seats. Peanut sellers and tea vendors jostled each other in the narrow passage of the compartment. Finally, the train started and rocked and rolled its way out of the city. The swirling fan kept the heat and the mosquitoes away and the metal windows were shut against the strong wind.

Early in the morning, the train approached their station, Tintodan. Vimla and Chintu lowered their bags onto the dusty platform, as a single porter appeared. He wore the trademark red bandana and red shirt and came forward to help them carry their stuff.

This was an entirely new place for Chintu. Away from fast-track Mumbai, time and his horses seemed to be taking a short nap here. Everything had slowed down. The station was quiet. The air was clear with a hint of dust. A couple of men greeted each other casually as they sauntered past. A dog trotted along the platform pawing a leftover piece of bread. And there, waiting at the small arched entrance of the station, was wiry Chhagan Dada, with black bushy eyebrows, no moustache and *dhoti* in place. The station was almost empty.

'How are you, daughter-in-law?' said Chhagan Dada as they bent to touch his feet for his blessings. 'How was the journey? This must be Chintan! What a prince! The auto is outside. Here, let me take this bag. Your aunt is waiting for you. You must be starved.'

Chhagan Dada's reassuring chatter eased them as they jerked along the empty road in an auto rickshaw, as the sun rose overhead.

Tintodan. This was Chintu's first trip to Dada's village. The muddy roads were uneven with cracks on the surface. It was already beginning to get hot and there was a haze of dust over the scraggly trees with white and orange rings painted on their bark. The rickshaw overtook two bullock carts that ambled along at an unhurried pace. Chintu's night in the train was like a bridge between the two worlds.

Chhagan Dada introduced the new sights as they bounced along.

'Our village used to be the pride of this district. The old raja built that rest house for travellers.' They followed his finger to the ruins of a building that still had a few remnants of its past glory. 'No-one could maintain it after he died. And there . . .' he pointed to a long, muddy depression in the ground, 'is the old lake, Tintodan Talao. It used to provide water for all our needs.' Chintu looked hard. 'But there's hardly any water in it now.' Chhagan Dada sighed.

'Ah yes, the water levels have fallen.' He looked up at the sky. 'No rains yet. Every year it gets worse. Of course the government gives us running water in taps now, but it runs away four days a week!' He guffawed at his own joke. 'We're lucky to have our own well.'

The auto stopped outside a small whitewashed house, like the ones Chintu had seen in his storybooks, with a small courtyard in front. In the corner of the courtyard was a small well with a pulley to lift buckets of water. In the centre was a white pedestal with a small, sacred Tulsi plant potted inside it. Behind this was a long balcony with a number of rooms that opened up onto it. There was a separate section on the left and the aromas that emerged from it told them that it was the kitchen. It was large, rambling and very different from the cramped flats Chintu had seen in Mumbai.

'Come, you can wash your feet here. There is some water and a mug in this bucket. The road is so dusty. Yes, leave your slippers on the steps. Inside it's cool. The toilet's over there. It's a pukka, strong brick one we made last year. Come Chintu. I'll show you the terrace where you can fly kites.'

While his mother went off to the kitchen to greet Dadi, Chintu explored the house. There was a ground floor and a first floor, connected by steep, narrow wooden steps. The rooms were small and dark. One room contained a big carved wooden trunk with a brass lock. Chhagan Dada told him that such trunks used to contain the family's wealth, and they were made broader than the door's width, so that they could not be pulled outside by thieves. Now that the wealth had been distributed, this trunk only contained the larger cooking vessels. There was also a basement. 'This was to hide valuables in, when there were raids by enemy soldiers,' Chhagan Dada explained. Part of the first floor had a terrace with grey cement flooring. They used to fly kites here. The house had a lot of history and a bit of mystery too.

'And here's Maahi, my granddaughter.'

A slim girl about Chintu's age in a red flowered dress and one braid stepped out from behind the kitchen door and walked quickly to the courtyard well.

'Maahi, here's Chintu, Mansukh Dada's grandson. You can show him around the village. This is his first visit here.'

She gave a sideward glance at Chintu and proceeded to dunk the bucket into the well till it hit the water with a distant splash. *Maahi*, thought Chintu. *My cousin! How come no one mentioned her to me!*

She pulled the bucket up, swung it expertly onto the ground and carried it to the kitchen with smooth, practiced movements. A brown and white cat followed her inside.

Chhagan Dada sat on the wide platform in front of the house. Chintu watched fascinated, as he picked a thin twig from a bundle and began chewing on it.

'Are her parents coming for the *pooja*?' Vimla asked politely.

'Well, my dear, they can't make it. My son is travelling for work. But Maahi stays here with us. Now that our sons don't live in the village any more, they leave their children safely with their grandparents. Better jobs in the cities, you know.' He rubbed the chewed end of the twig up and down his teeth. Then he paused to ask, 'And what about my nephew, your husband, Vishnu? Doing well in Dubai, eh?'

Mother adjusted her saree *pallu*.

'Oh yes! He's working hard and piling up gold for Chintu's future wife, I hope!' They both laughed comfortably.

Dadi called from the kitchen. 'Are you still brushing your old teeth? Wash your mouth now, breakfast is on its way!'

Chhagan Dada chuckled as he threw the chewed up twig into the henna bush behind the house.

'This is the best toothbrush ever! This is a neem twig, Chintu. It's bitter, but its juice keeps away all diseases.'

They washed their hands as Maahi appeared with a copper pot.

'Good child, this girl. Maahi has been with us for a few years now. She knows all our ways and is a great help. She makes our annual stock of mango pickles with her grandmother up on the terrace. Next year, her parents will take her away with them to Ahmedabad. She will go to a good school there.'

Chintu sat cross-legged on the flagged passage outside the kitchen with his mother and Chhagan Dada. The girl served them sweet tea and freshly roasted *khakhra* with ghee and a red masala on steel plates. Dadi supervised from a stool. They chatted amiably as Chintu warily watched the two lizards on the opposite wall, and the spider hanging from a faded old curtain.

He had little to say, except to answer the usual questions about school. Then, they got up and washed their hands into a bucket while the girl poured water.

'Maahi, take Chintu and show him around.'

Maahi put the water mug down and walked to the door. Chintu silently followed her out of the hall into the sunlight. They walked to the compound wall and she jumped neatly up onto the parapet. He joined her. The brown and white cat jumped quietly up beside Maahi and curled her tail. For a while, no one spoke. Then, she half-turned to him.

'How tall is your house?'

Chintu was startled by her question.

'It has six floors. We live on the first floor.'

She finally glanced up at him. 'Only six? Dadu told me in Mumbai the buildings touch the sky.'

'Who's Dadu?'

'Grandfather.'

'Oh. Is that what you call him? I call my grandfather Dada.'

Chintu was beginning to feel like a prince from an exotic land. It was obvious his cousin had never been far from her village.

'Well,' he continued, 'Some buildings are like that. But . . . er . . . their lifts are so crowded. I prefer smaller buildings. A six-storey building is perfect.'

They settled themselves in the shade of the low parapet wall of the courtyard. It was already beginning to get hot.

Chintu inquired, 'Why don't you stay with your parents in Ahmedabad?'

She shrugged her shoulders.

'They have to get settled and save money before I can go there to a big school. I'll go next year.'

'Don't you miss them?'

'She looked down. 'Sometimes.'

Chintu couldn't imagine living away from his mother. Dada would be there, but he would still miss her.

'Why do you have to get water from the well? You have taps.'

She turned her head away casually. 'We only get water sometimes. Like two or three times a week. Sometimes even less.'

Only twice or thrice a week! They would be dry cleaning themselves five times a week without the well water!

'Oh. Don't you have regular baths?'

She didn't answer but looked aslant at him as if she was sizing him up. Then she jumped up, her black oiled braid swinging. 'I'll show you the gap in the toilet wall. Come on!'

Weird girl! Gap in the toilet wall! What a village showpiece for him!

He and the cat followed her to the back of the toilet, adjoining the compound wall.

'Look.'

He strained his head to see the small gap at the earthen bottom of the toilet's brick wall. It was just a gap, and the smell was not very pleasant.

'So what? It's just a gap.' He bent to peer closer. 'What's so special?'

'Snake. Cobra.'

'Aiiiiyeeeeeeeeee!' Chintu pulled his head out of the gap and fell over backwards, grazing his cheek. The cat screeched, turned a somersault and fled at Chintu's cry.

'Shhhhhhhhh!'

'You fool!'

'Stop yelling!'

'A c . . . c . . . cobra! Where??'

'Stop it! Sissy! It's not here now. It doesn't come every day!'

'S . . . S . . . Sissy? You just want me to get b . . . b . . . bitten by your cobra and d . . . d . . . die! Then you won't need to f . . . f . . . fetch water for me!'

She hid her mouth behind her hand, but her eyes laughed at him.

'A little pot is soon hot!'

'Sh . . . sh . . . shut up! What do you mean?'

'Nothing. You're just a scared city boy!'

'City boys don't have p . . . poisonous snakes and s . . . scorpions crawling around their a . . . ankles!'

She did not respond but still hid her mouth behind her hand.

'Listen you haven't even been to the c . . . c . . . city and you think you know so much! We have theatres, b . . . big malls, shops, Internet c . . . cafes . . .'

Maahi shrugged. 'Everyone thinks his own ducks are swans. And why are you stammering?'

Oh no! She had frightened him. Time to breathe. Breathe deeply. One, two, three . . .

'You frightened her.'

'Who?'

'Mishty. My cat.'

'Who c . . . c . . . cares.'

Chintu walked off. Was she a female Bagadia, bent on teasing him? Well he would avoid her.

It was easy to stay away from Maahi. Preparations for the *pooja* were under way. Chintu went with Chhagan Dada to fetch provisions for the house, Dadi and Vimla visited the temple where their family always worshipped. They had already invited the village people. Now, fruits and sweetmeats, vessels and other odds and ends had to be bought. It was hot. They walked along the only road in the village and Chhagan Dada greeted people on the way, reminding them about the *pooja*.

Chintu wanted to find out as much as he could about his blood relatives, but he soon realized that mother would be better at that. There was general talk about the rising price of food grains, the new municipal councillor and the illness of an elderly relative. The morning seemed long, but there was no useful information.

At lunch time, Dadi sat down heavily on a small round stool in the kitchen and supervised Maahi while she served them.

'The *dhoklas* are hot. Eat them quickly. There's plenty of this delicious mango chutney with fried potatoes as well. Eat well. Sleep this afternoon. You must be tired,' she said as she patted Chintu's head.

Chintu couldn't help liking her. She was comfortably round. His own grandmother might have been like her. Dadi's legs were swollen and she walked from side to side with a rocking motion, but her sharp eyes noticed any empty spaces on their plates and Maahi was instructed to serve everything twice over.

Everyone slept that afternoon. Chintu slept through the tinkling of the ice-cream man on his cycle, the beggar lady in wild clothes and woke to the barking of the local dogs who had decided to have a quick fight. It was already 5.30 p.m. and his mother was in the kitchen with Dadi.

He couldn't find Maahi but she appeared at dinner time. They ate early.

'Chintu, help me sort out these packets of sugar cubes. We are giving them away to the *pooja* guests.' Vimla was in the courtyard filling up tiny bags through which the square sugar pieces could be seen.

'Mother, did you find out anything? Did you tell Chhagan Dada?'

Mother separated a pile of bags that were filled.

'I heard lots of new names and gossip which I can go back and tell Dada. But what can I tell Chhagan Dada? That we are searching for a needle in a haystack because 40 years ago, someone made a vague prediction? How would I know who is going to help the village!' She began filling a small sack with the bags. 'Still, I like it here.'

On Sunday morning, Chintu went out with Chhagan Dada again. He needed clues. What clues could he find? He didn't know anyone. He didn't know what to say. Who would take him seriously?

Could he learn something from Maahi? He was still annoyed with her. She was more worried about her silly cat than about frightening him. Still there was something different about her.

Chintu discovered Maahi had a full routine even though she had holidays from school like him. Apart from drawing water, she hung up the clothes to dry in the courtyard after the washerwoman had left. She also sorted out the vegetables and plucked the stems of coriander into a neat bunch. Before meal times, she was in the kitchen with Dadi and in the evenings she delivered the dried clothes for ironing to the washerman who lived three lanes away. Dadi couldn't do these things. Her legs were usually swollen.

'She has gas in her legs.'

'What?? How can you have gas in your legs? Do they fart?'

She hid her mouth behind her hand but her shoulders shook with amusement. 'You don't understand anything!' she said before she ran off.

Maahi was a big help to Dadi. She always closed the gate after entering or leaving, or the stray cows and goats got in and ate the plants in the courtyard. But she didn't talk much.

'Well what do you all DO here?' Chintu asked that evening. They were sitting perched on the parapet wall and the sun was low on the horizon. 'The electricity goes off any time, so you can't watch TV. You go to bed at 8.30 or 9.00 p.m. Don't you do anything besides pulling water, sorting vegetables and hanging the clothes out?'

Maahi looked away. She rarely looked at him directly. She swung her legs under her pink skirt and looked at the sky.

'Well what do you all do in Mumbai? Don't you wash your clothes and eat?'

'Silly! We do lots of other stuff. Mummy goes to work in an office and Dada works on the computer at home. In school, we have an inter-school competition for a school project and I'm on the water committee. If we win, Aamir Khan will shake hands with us!'

Maahi had seen Aamir Khan in a movie last year when

her parents had come from Ahmedabad and taken her as a special treat. She remembered his intense twinkling eyes and his mouth that could curve itself into the happiest of smiles, or turn down in a scowl.'

For a moment, Maahi struggled between jealousy, wonder and the image of Aamir Khan.

'Does he live in Mumbai?'

'Of course. Quite close to my house. I've even seen him go by in his car once.'

She overcame her shyness.

'Does he look as nice in real life?'

'Well he looks okay, but he's fair and has nice eyes.'

She sighed.

'What do you do in your water committee?'

Chintu spent the next hour telling Maahi about the competition while Maahi stroked Mishty's fur. Time flowed by smoothly as he described the different conservation projects. The other stories crept in too, until he found himself telling Maahi about Gopal Bagadia, Miss Reena and the challenge of the pouch.

'You mean your Muscles teacher didn't know that your friend was cutting the cord around his neck while he was upside down in his yoga pose?' Her laughter emerged as a series of giggles, her mouth hidden behind her hand.

'No, he was talking all the time, explaining to Arjun how to do it, and I ran off with the pouch like a tiger was chasing me!'

'Or a cobra!' she giggled again and swung her legs.

'Why do you laugh with your hand in front of your mouth? Will the cobra bite your tongue?'

She became serious immediately. She looked down.

'Dadi says I shouldn't show my teeth.'

'Why, what happened to them?'

She spluttered with hidden laughter again.

'Nothing! Don't you know it's rude to laugh with your teeth showing?'

Chintu only gave her a wry look. He was slowly realizing that people here had such different ways! They still lived so much in the way Dada must have lived here many years ago. And away in Mumbai, Chintu had a faster life where every day brought new events, new challenges, and the night came before he was ready for it. Yes, that train journey from Mumbai to Tintodan was like a bridge between two worlds in different time zones.

In the two days that he had been here, he was beginning to talk more freely with this newly discovered cousin. In fact, he realized that she could be his greatest ally in his quest for the saviour. Could he tell her straightaway? He wasn't sure how to begin. They got onto the parapet and sat with their backs to the house. The darkness would descend slowly. The still air was filling with the flapping and chirping of returning birds. The heat was less fierce.

'I'd better go and help Dadi with the cooking.'

'Wait. Do you believe in predictions?'

'Predictions?'

'Yes, like how an astrologer predicts things.'

'Oh, you mean like when the Pandit*ji* comes and matches the boy's birthdate and horoscope papers with the girl's horoscope before they can get married?'

'It's a bit like that but more. It's like someone tells you

what's going to happen in your life because it's all decided beforehand. And it's even written down.'

Maahi frowned and plucked at her skirt.

'I don't know. Dadi called in our Pandit*ji* before her sister's niece got married last year and he matched the horoscopes and said they would be very happy together. But Dadi says since they got married, they've been fighting all the time. I don't know.'

'Well a *Chhaaya Shaastri* made some predictions about Dada and I've come here to find someone from his family who is going to help the village with water.'

For the first time, Maahi looked straight into Chintu's eyes.

'What?'

Chintu told her about the predictions made when Dada was a young man, Dadi's illness, Dada's search on Facebook for the possible saviour from the family. Maahi listened carefully, silently, and Chintu's story overflowed into the last prediction that he had read while Dada snored quietly on his pillow. The prediction that Dada's 67th year might be his last.

Maahi looked up. She was breathing faster and there were small beads of sweat on her upper lip.

'And you say lots of this has come true already?'

'Yes, almost all the main things, till now.'

Maahi looked at him as if she was debating something.

'Did he say how the village would benefit? Did he say water would come to each house every day through the taps? Will the fields have tomatoes and corn and groundnuts growing the way they used to?

'I don't know. He only said the village would benefit through water. Why are you asking me all this?'

She glanced at him, almost as if she was sizing him up for the first time. Finally she said in a low voice, 'There is something. I haven't told anyone except my friend Neha. I don't know if I should tell you. '

All of Chintu's senses came alive. 'What? What is it?'

She bit her lip. 'You don't live here so it won't matter to you if you know or not.'

'Well, tell me anyway! Is it about what I told you?'

'I don't know, I don't know! And you're only here for three more days!'

'Well say something! You can't just say "I don't know" like that!'

She wrung her hands for a few moments and looked towards the kitchen.

She called out, 'Dadi, can I show Chintu the small Svayambhu temple by the cow enclosure? We'll be back very soon.'

'Make sure you are back before it's dark,' came the reply.

'Alright!' she called back. Then to Chintu, 'Come on, quick! I have to show you something.'

She ran to a corner of the courtyard where a pile of wood was stacked. She pulled out a twig with two ends, like a fork and raced out. Chintu ran after her. Was this another snake-trick? There was something strange about this girl, even if she was friendlier than yesterday. Whatever it was, he kept pace behind her.

The sun was low on the horizon as they ran. Past the dry old well, past the temple where the idol was found buried beneath the ground, past the enclosure where old cows lived together. They sped past the dusty wild thorn bushes and the darkening Babul trees, across the cracked and pale ground, which sloped down to a wide, flat stump of an old banyan tree cut down years ago. Maahi stopped abruptly and panted as she gripped her twig. She held it tightly with both hands, one end of the fork part in each hand with her palms and forearms facing skywards.

'What are you do . . .'

'Shhhhh! Just watch.'

Chintu adjusted his glasses. In the darkening half-light, Maahi positioned her twig and began a slow walk towards the tree stump on which Chintu was now sitting. The sun was sinking in a bed of dark red. The rustling trees behind her waved their thin arms and the ground reflected their long, black shadows.

She walked slowly, deliberately, with the fork of the twig grasped firmly in her upturned palms. About halfway from the stump, a strange thing began to happen. The twig in her hand began to move. The bent end of the twig quivered. Then it began to rotate slowly, slowly, inwards towards Maahi's body until after a few steps, it had turned halfway round from its first position and was pointing to the ground.

It had moved by itself.

Chintu felt a queer shiver go up his spine. He sprang up, away from Maahi.

'Stop it! Just s . . . s . . . stop this nonsense! Why are you turning the twig? Are you t . . . t . . . trying to frighten me? Are you trying some b . . . b . . . black magic or something?' He was shaking a bit now, in the approaching darkness and this strange place and this mysterious girl.

'Shhh! Stop it! It's okay, don't shout! I'm just showing you something. I'm not doing anything, it's happening by itself! That's what I wanted to show you.'

'I don't b . . . b . . . believe you. You're trying to s . . . s . . . scare and trick me and then l . . . l . . . laugh at me!'

'Oh just listen, will you! It's not bad magic!'

They were whispering fiercely, and the darkness was slowly beginning to hide their faces.

'Listen, I didn't know about this place myself! This just happens to me every time I pass this spot with a forked twig in my hand!' She came closer.

'K . . . k . . . keep away from me! Go away! You are w . . . w . . . weird!'

'Chintu, do you know what this means?'

'I don't c . . . c . . . care, I'm g . . . g . . . going back home now.'

'But just listen . . .'

'S . . . s . . . stop it, stop! I don't want to h . . . h . . . hear anything! I'm going!' He hesitated. 'Are you c . . . c . . . coming?'

'Of course I'm coming!' She looked serious. 'Don't be scared. You're scaring me now.'

Chintu stumbled back home in the gloom behind Maahi, shaking inside and out. It was weird. What did that mean? How did that stick turn by itself? Weird, weird! Everything was weird, the village, their ways, the darkness and this girl with her rotating twig. *His cousin.* What did it all mean?

At dinner, Vimla ate quietly. She had been helping Dadi and learning new dishes. She noticed Chintu's silence and thought it best to leave him alone. A new place could be unsettling at first, but she had seen him chatting with Maahi in the courtyard. He would soon adjust to this place. In any case they would be back in Mumbai in three days.

All her chats with Chhagan Dada and the relatives at the temple had brought her up-to-date with the members of the bloodline, but how could she know who the 'saviour' was going to be? Would it be the richest man and would he give lots of money for a fancy water pump? Would that quench the thirst of the dried fields and bring water regularly to each home? Or would it be some expert with the knowledge of how to harness water? She had no idea. The best she could do was to go home and report to Dada the latest gossip about the members of his bloodline. He could take it from there.

That Sunday night, in the open courtyard and under the twinkling stars that looked closer than they did in Mumbai, Maahi told Chintu her strange story of the turning stick.

15

THE WATER DIVINER

'Hello? Hello? Nandu bhaiyya?'

'Hello?'

'Hello, Nandu bhaiyya?'

'Yes, this is Nandu. Who's that? Chintu?'

'Yes, Nandu bhaiyya, it's Chintu! Listen, I have lots to tell you!'

'Chintu, is everything okay? It's Monday morning and I'm leaving for the office now. Dada's fine. What's happening?'

'Arre Nandu bhaiyya! I've f . . . found her! She knows where the water is but she c . . . c . . . can't tell anyone. She showed me. She's weird but she's okay. I'm telling you she's the one! The one we're looking for!'

'Hold on, hold on, breathe deeply! Now tell me calmly what's happening. Where's your mum?

'She's coming in a minute. She wants to talk to you. But Nandu bhaiyya we've found her! What do we do now? We can't just tell everybody, nobody will believe her.'

'Chintu, can you say one word at a time? I don't understand . . .'

'Okay here's Ma.' Vimla took over. Chintan listened excitedly to her side of the conversation.

'Nandu, how's Dada? Good. Give him our respects. Yes. Chintu was trying to tell you about it. It's Chintu's cousin, Maahi. MAAHI. Yes . . . She can feel the presence of water under the ground. Yes . . . yes she does it with a twig. A TWIG. A twig shaped like a fork. Yes. Yes. She showed Chintu. She holds the twig and the twig bends towards the ground by itself in her hand as she walks . . . Yes, it bends where the water is, under the ground. Yes . . . I know, it sounds strange. Yes. Chintu told me about it, and she took us both to the same spot and she showed me too. Yes, I saw it too. Yes, it happens. No, she's not doing it. It happens by itself. Yes, yes, I made sure of that. No, she found this spot a year ago . . . No, she hasn't told anyone except her friend. She's scared . . . She's too young and people here might think it's some kind of bad magic. Yes. Yes. But Nandu I don't know if there's really water there! She says she and her mother used to do this in her earlier village. When the twig turned, that spot was drilled. They usually found water there. Have you ever heard of anything like this? It might mean anything!

How can we find out? No . . . No, she doesn't know how deep the water is below the ground. And even if we knew, what could we do?'

There was a short pause. Then the line crackled again.

'Okay, call me back in two hours. Bye.' She turned to Chintu. 'He'll ask some people and check it out. We have to call back in two hours.'

'But what will he check?'

'I don't know, but Nandu will figure it out.'

Vimla got up. They had been sitting on the same tree stump in the same secluded spot where Maahi had showed Chintu the wonder of the bending twig, the evening before.

Vimla had been astounded by Chintu's story the night before. She thought the whole story was crazy. Chintu wanted her to see how it happened, so this morning, Maahi, Chintu and she had come to the spot. Maahi had walked over the same spot and again, the twig bowed to the presence of water underneath. Yes, she saw it too. The twig had turned towards the ground by itself.

All her life, Vimla's parents had believed in science. Things that you couldn't clearly explain were usually considered silly. But now she had seen this with her own eyes.

'Chintya, I really don't know what to think about all this! If I hadn't seen it myself, I wouldn't have believed it. I'm puzzled myself. She said her mother taught her. How did she and her mother do this? She says if the twig bends, it means there is water under the ground! If this is true, all kinds of plans can be made for the village and Dada will be so happy! Anyway, I know Nandu will find some kind of solution. He always does.' She looked at her watch. 'Oh, time to go. I have to go to the temple for an hour. I'll meet you here at noon. Don't be late. We have to be back for lunch by 1 p.m.' She left.

Chintu walked homewards. His mind was still whirling after the story Maahi had told him last night. He remembered their talk with the stars twinkling clearly above them.

'But is it a magic twig? Where did you find it?' he had asked.

Maahi raised her hand to hide her laughter again. 'Of course it's not a magic twig! It's just an ordinary piece of wood shaped like a fork!'

'But how can YOU know how to feel water under the ground? You're just . . . you're just . . . a girl!' he had exclaimed after listening to her.

She turned on him immediately. 'Only a girl! That's what people say, "Only a girl!" They think a girl can't do such things! That's why I'm afraid to tell anyone! But my name is Maahi. It's the name of a river. And you know that most rivers in our country have female names?'

Chintu digested this.

'But how do you know it's to do with water?'

'My mother showed me,' she said quietly.

'Your mother? Does she know how to do the same thing? Has she done it too?'

'Of course. I did it with her. And we usually found water.'

She put her hand over her mouth and her shoulders shook with laughter. 'Sometimes it was dirty, brackish water and the landowners shouted at us!'

'But you said three bore wells were drilled in Tintodan

and they didn't find water! How come you feel the water's under that spot there?'

Maahi looked down and spoke softly. 'Did you see the land there? It slopes down. Water always flows to the lower ground.'

'Arre, but the water's underground!'

'Wherever it is, it always flows down. That bit of land is the lowest. Even underground water will flow there unless it's trapped.'

How did she know all this? Just by living in the village and observing things around her?

Chintu had already begun to see Maahi as someone different, someone with magic flowing through her, like the water of many rivers, as if she was born from the female bloodline of rivers.

All that happened last night. Today was Monday, and as he turned into the gate of the whitewashed house, he was still thinking about it all. He latched the gate and turned to find Maahi with flowers in her shining long braid, hanging up the clothes to dry.

'Maahi, we called Nandu bhaiyya. He'll do something. Remember I told you how he helped me with the bully Bagadia in my school?'

Maahi bit her lip. 'I don't want to tell anyone. Father always said there were nine virtues in silence.'

'Don't worry so much! You'll be a hero! Or heroine! But how do you know there's water under the ground? The twig might be bending for some other reason.'

'You are always asking questions! Questions and answers don't walk around in pairs like you think! Some answers come by themselves. I have to go now.' She ran, disappearing into the smoky kitchen. She would not come out for an hour now.

Why did Maahi speak in riddles? thought Chintu as he made his way back to the water spot before noon. Ma was waiting at the stump of the banyan tree. They called up Nandu bhaiyya.

'Hello? Nandu? Yes. So what happened?'

There was a pause as she listened to the crackling voice over the mobile phone.

'What? Water what? Water diviner? Did you say WATER DIVINER? What's that? Something divine like an angel or goddess? Oh. Not divine, but DIVINER? You googled it? Oh. Oh you mean you looked it up on Google.com. Oh. Oh. Aha. Aha. OH! Really? You mean a WATER DIVINER is someone who can tell that there's water under a particular spot on the ground? Aha. Is there such a thing? But what will we do? Are you sure? Look, Nandu, I have to go to office and Chintu has school. Yes, yes, but we don't know if it's really just some nonsense . . . Yes I'm sure I saw it. Yes, it happens. It happened every time. Yes. Yes. Okay we'll wait. Day after tomorrow. Okay. Listen, I hope it's not a waste of time. Okay. We'll call again tomorrow. Okay. Bye.'

She hung up and turned to Chintu. 'Chintu, I don't know what's happening, but Nandu is coming here day after tomorrow, on Wednesday.'

'What? Here? Why? What will he do? Wednesday is the day of the *pooja*, the day we leave.'

Vimla sat quietly with her hands on her lap.

'I hope we are not going to create some kind of storm here, but Nandu wants to see this himself. He says it's important.

And in case you have forgotten, your school contest is in less than three days, on Thursday. Do you want to wait here longer with Nandu or go back day after tomorrow as we had planned?'

The school contest! Everything came back to him in a flash. Arjun, Miss Reena, Muscles Sir, Bully Bagadia, Principal Shashi, the water project . . .

'Aamir Khan!' he exclaimed in dismay. 'I have to meet him! We have to go back!'

Vimla began to say something, then changed her mind. 'Alright. Nandu can stay on. We'll go back after the *pooja*, on Wednesday night, as planned. Our train leaves late. We'll get home very early on Thursday morning.'

That night, Chintu's head streamed with thoughts. So she was a *Water Diviner.* He had seen it happen. The twig bent by itself, every time. Maahi had explained it all simply. Her mother was a water diviner too. In her mother's village, people asked her to help them find water before they tried digging or drilling wells on the dry land. Maahi had told him that people could waste a lot of money drilling without knowing where to find water. Whenever they asked Maahi's mother, they usually found water under the ground where the twig turned and near the spot she pointed out. This saved them money and time and then they could grow crops by channelling the water to the land. She and her mother had tried with the twig together when she was just seven years old. The twig had bent for her too.

And now, Nandu bhaiyya was coming. Surely something very interesting would happen. The main thing was that they had found her. He fell asleep with that thought.

16

PREPARATIONS

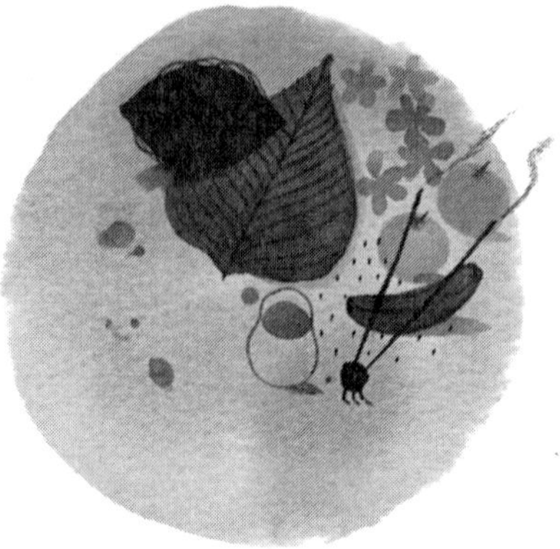

Sunday and Monday had produced more questions that Chintu wanted to ask Maahi, but she was at Dadi's beck and call. Besides, she seemed to avoid Chintu. She went away in the afternoon for half an hour to apply henna designs on her hands. The grand *pooja* was tomorrow, and that evening, they would leave. Ma spent most of her time with Dadi in the kitchen where other ladies from the neighbourhood had also congregated. They cleaned the rice and wheat grains which would be cooked for the *pooja* lunch, checked the provisions and made the sweets.

Chhagan Dada took Chintu with him, to buy fruit and various items that the pandit needed for the *pooja*.

'Pandit*ji* will make me buy the whole shop, at this rate!' He read out from a piece of notepaper with tiny writing on it.

'Coconut, betel leaves, vermilion powder, fruit, incense sticks and the silver pot for the water. Hmph! I will have to get that from the silversmith.'

'Can't we use the clay pot you have at home?'

'No, my four-eyed prince, we need a silver one. Silver doesn't allow bacteria to settle on the water and it's a natural sterilizer. It's to hold the water that will wash the idol so we need purity, my dear! Silver and water for cleanliness.'

'Oh.'

Water. And he was head of the school water committee! Somehow water seemed to have become the most important thing in his life. School seemed so far away from here.

Excitement was in the air. People greeted each other on the road and spoke only about the next day's *pooja*. It was to begin at 10 a.m. and go on for two hours. Chintu's train was to leave only at 8 p.m. They shopped and visited Pandit*ji* at the temple. Chintu's bare feet felt cool on the white marble floor and he felt very peaceful.

And tomorrow Nandu bhaiyya was coming.

17

A SURPRISE GUEST ARRIVES

The early morning light was still pale when Chintu woke up to the sound of muffled voices outside in the courtyard. There were many voices and a rickshaw and sounds of things being dragged around. Chintu flung off the sheet that covered him and ran out. Nandu bhaiyya had arrived!

'Nandu bh . . .' his words stuck as he realized there were four other people with Nandu bhaiyya including a fair young girl. Luggage was piled up all around, filling the small courtyard. A medium-sized white van was parked in the corner near the well. It had a satellite dish hooked up on its top, like a metal moon. Chhagan Dada chatted with everyone at the same time, pulling out two wooden bedframes bound with cloth strips for everyone to sit on. Slowly they arranged themselves on the bed and Dadi rocked her way to the kitchen to make everyone some hot tea.

'So, Chintya, we made it here! And I have brought some of my colleagues too. We are going to check out this story of yours.' Nandu held out some chocolates he had bought in the train. Chintu was suddenly tongue-tied. What was happening? Why so many people? He silently accepted the chocolates.

Nandu turned to his friends.

'Chhagan Dada says we can stay at the temple's guesthouse and also have our meals there. That will be convenient for us to set up the filming equipment and I've hired this autorickshaw for the whole day. Our overhead broadcasting van has everything we need. We can use the generator near the filming spot if we muffle the noise.'

Film equipment? Filming spot? What was going on?

'We'll go to the spot first, and check out all we need. Raju, can you check out all the line connections? We can't have the power going off in the middle of a live telecast.'

'Sure, Nandu. No problem.'

'Okay, and Viju, can you take over the audio equipment? We have the checklist so you just need to see everything's working.'

'Okay, boss! It'll just take a couple of hours.'

'Great! Ahh, here comes the tea! Dadi, you are a life saver! Guys, Dadi here is an excellent cook. I bet you've never tasted better tea.'

Dadi beamed and brought out some freshly roasted *khakhras*. 'And who is this girl? Is she also from the office? Is she married?' She looked keenly at the fair girl.

'Yes Dadi, this is Pheroza. We call her Phizzy. And she's not married!'

Phizzy moved up and gave Dadi a hug. 'These *khakhras* are delicious, Dadi! Can you teach me to cook?'

'Of course! Stay with me and I will teach you everything. Your future husband will be happy.' There was some teasing laughter directed at Phizzy which she took good naturedly.

'And now, Chintu, where is your cousin Maahi? She's going to be the star of our show!'

Maahi? Suddenly everything clicked in Chintu's mind. All this was to film Maahi! Maahi, the water diviner! He had told Nandu all about the strange way she could feel where water was under the ground. They would film Maahi. They would film the mysterious bending of the twig near underground water!

Chintu watched as the crew moved around the small courtyard. All this was completely sudden and unexpected. Nandu bhaiyya hadn't told them about filming Maahi. How would they manage it all?

He could picture the headlines: 'Mysterious Moments!' or 'The Twig Bows to Water!' TV Channel 16 was going to film the water divining! Nandu bhaiyya's office people were the filming crew. He had brought all the equipment they needed and people would be able to see the way the twig turned downwards at the place where water flowed under the ground. So that's what it was all about! It was a big thing. Maahi would be on TV! How would she feel? Maybe this was her big chance. Maybe she could even meet Aamir Khan, if she became famous.

Nandu had worked feverishly to make all this possible. He had done his research. Not many people knew about water divining. It was a new story, and if all went well this story would attract a large audience. It might even mean a promotion.

Nandu's friend had struck a deal with the owner of a pump-making company to bring their company's most efficient pump. They would drill at the spot to see if there really was water there. They may have to drill 20, 50, 100 metres down or even more. The owner of the company had agreed to do this free of cost as he would be on TV, get free publicity and maybe sell more pumps.

Nandu turned to Chintu. 'Television coverage, Chintu! Let the excitement begin!'

Vimla beckoned urgently to Nandu from the side of the house. He strolled over. She whispered furiously into his ear.

'Nandu, I didn't know you would be doing a film shoot on this! You can't just come over and start filming this way! We have to ask for permission first! Chhagan Dada and Dadi don't know. Maahi's parents are away in Ahmedabad. They will panic! They don't know anything about her water divining over here! This is a village! Things don't work like they do in Mumbai. And Maahi has no idea at all! And besides, the *pooja* is happening this morning! Nandu I wish you had told me . . .' she was almost in tears as her voice trailed off.

Nandu patted her back and whispered, 'Don't worry, Aunty! I will work all that out and there will be no problem.

Just leave it to me and everyone will be delighted. In fact we will all smile over this historic day for the rest of our lives! Here, Aunty, breathe deeply once . . . twice . . . thrice . . . . good! Goodbye worries! Now I'll speak to Chhagan Dada and Dadi and then, tell me, where can I find this fascinating water diviner?'

Maahi was found. Nandu spirited Chhagan Dada and Dadi into a quiet room to talk to them and convince them it was alright to film everything. There was more talk and exclamations of surprise. But there was very little time. The *pooja* would start soon. After half an hour of steady talk by Nandu, they telephoned Maahi's parents in Ahmedabad. Another 15 minutes passed while voices crackled through the mobile phone. Finally Chhagan Dada emerged with excitement written all over his face. He had realized that he too would be on television as the grandfather of the water diviner. His mind was racing with possibilities.

'That land where the twig turns, belongs to Ramjibhai. He is a good man. He will be very happy if water is found on his land. He will surely share it with the whole village.'

He turned to Dadi. 'Eh, then, are you listening? Shall we pose together like we did on our wedding day? All our relatives will see us on television!'

'Hmphh. You can show the world your balding head if you like. I'm going to the *pooja*. Fifty years of our family temple, and you want to go off posing like a frolicking puppy for TV!' she replied.

Chhagan Dada chuckled. 'Look, Nandu said he would interview us after the *pooja*. We can be there for both events!'

'I'm not coming till the *pooja* is finished and everyone is fed.'

'We are all going to be with you, Dadi,' Vimla said. 'After all, we have come for this.'

Nandu patted Dadi. 'Well, Dadi, how do you feel being the grandmother of a true blue water diviner?'

Dadi was more subdued. 'Water divining, you say. It's not common nowadays, but I have sometimes heard of people doing this kind of thing with metal rods and coconuts. But why was she so afraid of telling anyone? If she was afraid of anything or anyone, I would have protected her!' She thought for a minute. 'Vimla, I don't like Maahi being on television and people gaping at her. We have a peaceful life here.' She waved her hands in the air. 'It's all too sudden. Besides, have you thought of what will happen if it doesn't work? It will be terrible!'

Chhagan Dada cut in. 'Arre think of all the good things that will come of it! If water is found, she will be praised and the village will have water! Isn't that a good thing?'

'And if there's no water? Who knows if her future in-laws will approve! Being on television and all that, like some film star!'

Nandu took over. 'Arre Dadi, she will be the star of the village and you will have pandits lining up with marriage offers from the most handsome young men, mark my words! Everyone is fascinated by a TV celebrity!'

'But what happens if there's no water there?'

'Don't worry, we are doing this as an experiment. Just seeing that twig turn by itself will be enough of a mystery for our viewers.'

Dadi shrugged. She felt uneasy. Her son in Ahmedabad was very excited and was all in support of the TV program. She wished she had more time to understand all that was happening. All these people from Mumbai rushed around doing things their way. Did they realize that others had lived for so many years, in a different way? Here, people asked permission. They talked things over with the elders and took their advice. Nandu seemed like a nice boy, but his way was not theirs. He was too young. His words were smooth but where was his experience? Perhaps this filming was good for his career, but did he know how everyone else felt about it? She said nothing but waddled off to the brick bathing area to bathe with the bucket of water Maahi had drawn. Her crisp new *pooja* sari was waiting.

The film crew left to set things up. The others were busy organizing themselves. Vimla's mind was whirling. She felt like she was on a see-saw, balancing the *pooja* and Nandu's sudden entry for his TV programme. Anyway, she knew Nandu's ways. He would manage somehow, while they performed the *pooja*. Chintu and Maahi were ready. Chhagan Dada was already in his whitest, freshest kurta set. It was time for the *pooja*.

They walked as a group towards the temple in the next lane. All the preparations had been made. The Pandit*ji* arrived and the musicians took their places. They settled themselves. Soon, relatives, friends, and neighbours began filling the marble temple. Greetings were exchanged and the *pooja* began.

The Lord of the temple was invoked and hands were folded.

'Chintan bhai, please offer this to the Lord,' Pandit*ji* plucked an apple from a big round silver plate and held it out. Chintu approached, took it and placed it gently in front of the marble figure. Turn by turn, Maahi, Vimla, Chhagan Dada and Dadi did the same. Pandit*ji* chanted some verses and the others repeated. Between the chanting, offerings were made to the sacred fire. The chanting began again. Dadi closed her eyes, her lips moving to the chants. As people joined in, the chanting echoed around the walls. An hour passed. The *pooja* was in full swing.

When the *pooja* had begun, half a kilometre away, at the stump of the banyan tree, the film crew was hard at work. There too, many preparations had to be made. Nandu was talking on his mobile to his Mumbai boss. Viju was sorting out wires. He and the cameraman were setting up a satellite link so that they could see and interview people who were in different parts of India. Phizzy, with Nandu's notes on her lap, was fiddling with some controls on a large, blinking box inside the overhead broadcasting van. The others were on their laptops, furiously working on their respective tasks.

'Is the satellite link working? Check the monitor, Viju.'

'Boss, we have a signal. It looks okay.'

'Great. Now let's go through the check list.'

Back in the gleaming marble interior of the temple, the chanting had given way to *bhajan* singing. Those who knew the prayer songs joined in, and the echoes rippled out from the temple compound. The drumming gave a beat to the *bhajans* and the people began to sway in rhythm. Dadi had closed her eyes and submitted to the echoing drums and singing.

At the filming site, Nandu was sitting on the tree stump, going through his checklist.

'Is the generator okay? We can't have the electricity going off in the middle of an interview!'

'It's all arranged.'

'And the interview questions? Phizzy?'

'Yes, Nandu, they're all sorted in this file.'

'Okay, thanks Phizzy. Now please fetch Chintu and Maahi. The *pooja* must be nearly over. Anyway, Dadi said they could leave the *pooja* a bit early if needed.'

'As you say boss.' Phizzy hurried off.

In the temple, the tempo of singing had picked up and people were clapping their hands in time to the beat. There were plates of fruit and sweets as offerings. Chhagan Dada and Dadi were sitting close to the Pundit, handing him the *pooja* items as he asked for them. Chintu and Maahi sat together at a slight distance.

Phizzy arrived and signalled to Chintu from the door, but he did not see her. She entered and picked her way across the crowded floor towards Chintu and Maahi.

'Chintu, Maahi, come on!' Chintu turned suddenly as Phizzy tapped him on his back. 'It's time now.'

They got up from the crowd. Maahi said nothing. The brown and white cat suddenly appeared beside her. It was strange walking away from that swaying, singing group with Phizzy. Chintu had forgotten himself in the singing, and he left in a daze, the rhythm of the singing still strong inside him. As they walked, Phizzy chattered excitedly about everything that was being prepared. They reached the stump of the tree.

'Here, Nandu, all ready to roll!'

Nandu turned round. 'Hey, Chintu, where's your cousin?'

They all turned. Maahi was nowhere to be seen.

18

DEB AND LI RETURN

Where was Maahi?

Chintu's heart began its drumming. He ran back, retracing his route. He thought of the different places he had seen with Maahi. The old dry well was deserted. The Svayambhu temple had a few people offering worship. Past the cow enclosure . . . wait, what was that shadow? It wasn't a cow. Chintu looked between the wide-set metal bars of the enclosure. There, between the broad flanks of two white cows lay Maahi, her arms spread helplessly along one cow's side, her head resting on it. Mishty was lying curled up on her lap.

'Maahi!'

She was startled and looked up briefly but did not reply.

'Maahi what are you doing with those cows? Come out!'

'Go away.'

'Oh come on now, you can't hide. I'm coming in.'

She said nothing as he lifted the hook over the metal ring on the gate and hurried in. The cows looked up and continued chewing.

'Everyone's looking for you! Nandu bhaiyya's waiting. You can show the world your water divining magic. You're going to be a star . . . I told you!'

She looked up. Her eyes were dull. Had she been crying?

'I heard everything. I don't want to be a star!'

'But don't you understand? You are the one we've been looking for! The one Dada's been looking for on Facebook! You're going to be the saviour of the village!'

She turned on him. 'YOU don't understand. Why did you tell everyone? I wish I hadn't told you! I thought I could tell you and you would go away in a few days and it would make no difference. But you made me show it to your mother and now your Nandu bhaiyya is here to make a film of it. I just want to live here quietly and go to Ahmedabad next year and be like other people!'

'But you are different! You're special! And you can be so useful to the village, don't you see?'

'I'm not special! I'm not even sure if there's water under that spot! I told you it usually works, but that doesn't mean always. If they don't find water, I'll be the laughing stock of the village! Have you thought of that?' she said in a voice muffled by tears.

Chintu was silent. It was true. She would never get over her fear that the twig initially showed where the water was, only later they would find that it wasn't there after all. The thumping in his chest speeded up. He adjusted his glasses, took a deep breath and bent down to speak to her.

'Maahi, even if there's no water, people will know about those who are water diviners. They need to see the stick turn, that's all. Then they'll know there are people like you in the world. Anyway, there's no need to be upset. Do what I tell you . . . breathe deeply. Breathe! Breathe with me.'

'What?'

'Just do what I'm saying. Don't ask. Breathe, breathe deeply. One . . . two . . . three . . . good. Again. One . . . two . . . three . . .' Better now? Things are never as bad as you think.' *Wow*, he thought, *that sounded like Abu Chacha.*

Maahi got up. She took another deep breath. She did feel better and also more determined.

'Go away now and leave me.'

'What? The cameras will start rolling in an hour! Come on! Come ON!' He held her arm and pulled.

She fought back fiercely. 'I didn't ask you to make me a star on TV! Just go away.' She hissed.

'Yes, but . . .'

'Just go.'

There was steel in her voice.

For the first time, Chintu felt the helplessness of the whole world. Here she was, she could be the saviour of her village! The great granddaughter of Dada's father, his bloodline, the target of all of Dada's searches. And she was a water diviner! She could mysteriously feel water under the earth. They could raise water from the ground and quench this land! There was so little time . . . ***In your 67th year, someone from your bloodline will benefit your village. The benefit will be connected with water in some way. That may also be the last year of your life.*** The words of the prophecy came back to him, the pieces of the jigsaw were falling in place and now, this saviour was refusing to do her magic!

She HAD TO come. What could he say to make her change her mind?

Chintu looked at her. She stood with her hands hanging down dejectedly. She looked like a normal girl with a shiny, long ribboned braid and flowered blouse and skirt. She went to school, helped her grandparents and shared her life with Mishty and the cows and snakes and lizards that also lived in the village. She was waiting for her parents to take her away to the big city. She had hidden her secret, and told him about it only because he was a stranger. He would go away. And now suddenly, her secret was being revealed to the whole world through the television. She was being turned upside down, like an overturned, helpless turtle, exposed, with no protection.

Chintu remembered Abu Chacha. He remembered DEB & LI. Do Everything Best & Leave It. *God helps you if you make your own efforts.* Chintu had made his efforts. He had come to Tintodan and seen this wonder. He had told his mother. They had called Nandu bhaiyya and now the film crew was here. How important it could be for Tintodan, for Dada, Chhagan Dada and Dadi, and her parents in Ahmedabad!

Yes, he had tried. Even here, amid the cows he had tried to convince Maahi. Now it was up to her. He could not force her, or protest any longer. He would have to leave it. *Perhaps the prophecy was not true after all.* He waited a moment, then turned and walked away slowly.

Soon, he disappeared from Maahi's line of sight.

She sat still, between the comforting calmness of the cows with Mishty purring on her lap. They sat under the shade of the trees. All around the enclosure, the pale brown land stretched to the edge of the old Tintodan Talao, where now, only small puddles of water remained. The dry heat hung in the air.

How had all this happened? She had kept her secret successfully. Her father had told her, 'There are nine virtues in silence'. So she had kept this secret too, to herself like a gem in a closed fist, until she opened her palm and showed her talent to this stranger from Mumbai. It had been snatched roughly out of her palm and now, they wanted to tell the whole world. It was like being in a storm with all your precious things blown about. This was not the way things were done, at least not here in Tintodan. And anyway, what did she understand about this secret herself? She did not know how it happened. She only knew that she had walked, copying her mother, holding the twig in both hands, thinking of water. She watched as the twig in her mother's hand bent easily at certain places. She had watched the drilling at the spot where the twigs bent. She had watched as water spurted from the ground. She found that the forked twigs she had picked had responded to her too, like a wet-nosed sniffing dog. She felt no tingling or electric shock when it bent. She only knew that when her twig bent, she felt in touch with the earth and the water beneath it.

Still, she could not face the camera.

She sighed, stroking Mishty's brown and white fur and looked up at the hot, cloudless sky. Something was pinging away in her head, like a knocking on a closed door. The pinging was trying to tell her something. What?

She looked around her. The monsoons rains should arrive in a few days. Yet look, the Keshudo trees were still dull. The flowers had not blossomed as they usually did, fiery bright red, a fortnight before the rains. The pinging grew louder. Some memory was coming back. Something that her mother had told her.

A rustling sound distracted her. She turned. There, under a bush near her feet in a hollow of scraped mud, was a nest. Her trained eyes looked for the source of the sound. There was a flash of brown and black wings. The Titodi bird! And its nest was on the ground! Ping! Ping! Oh! Oh! Was that it? Her mother had told her about the Titodi bird. It could sense if there was going to be a lot of rain, or very little. If she made her nest in the trees, there would be a lot of rain. If the nest was close to the ground, it meant the bird had no fear of rainwater washing its nest away. The bird's instinct was telling her that the monsoons would bring very little rain. Again. And the rains would be late.

The rains can't fail us this time, she thought. *Not again.* Ever since she had come to live in Tintodan, the rains had failed. Did she have unlucky feet? Pandit*ji* had told them a story about women who brought misfortune wherever their feet stepped. She could not bear the thought that she was one of them.

And then, it struck her. The Keshudo tree, the Titodi bird were all telling her something. They were telling her something *now, at this very moment.*

They were telling her that the monsoons would be late. The village needed water urgently and could not afford another bad monsoon. They were asking for her help. Could she help? If they found water where her twig turned, everyone would benefit and they would not be so badly affected by the poor monsoon rains.

They were telling her that she had to try.

Like a flash, her mother's words came back to her.

One fool can cause a whole shipwreck.

She would be a fool not to even try. Maybe she was chosen to prevent disaster. Maybe this was meant to happen. Maybe this cousin was meant to come and learn her secret. Maybe the prophecy was true after all.

Surely there WAS water under the spot near the stump of the banyan tree. The twig turned every time she walked there. She blinked and looked down. She would have to go through with it now and take the chance. She would face the camera and do her divining. The cows raised their heads as she got up and walked to the metal gate. Mishty yawned, stretched and followed.

19

THE DRAMA UNFOLDS

'WHERE IS SHE?' Nandu whispered fiercely to Chintu. 'You were supposed to bring her here! The TV coverage is starting now!'

'She won't come.'

'WHAT?'

'I tried everything, but she refused to come. I'm really sorry.'

Nandu sat down heavily on the ground.

'All my hard work . . . My TV show . . . what will I say? We go on air in two minutes. The borewell people are here with the rig. I'll lose my job. No one will hire me again . . .'

Chintu was shocked. He had never seen Nandu bhaiyya like this before.

'Breathe, Nandu bhaiyya, breathe! Things are never that bad, remember? Breathe with me. One . . . two . . . three . . . four . . . that's right!'

Nandu's lips had turned pale, but he breathed deeply. 'Okay, Chintu. Got to think fast. Go try to bring her here.'

He got up and called out to another man. 'Viju! Viju, have you got the other interviews ready? Good, we'll interview Ramjibhai first.'

'Hurry, boss, there's 30 seconds left.

Nandu took one of the deepest breaths he had taken in a long time. He took the microphone and walked up to the camera man just as Viju signalled. He put on a brave, smiling face.

'Welcome, viewers to this edition of Channel 16's daily news show. My name is Nandu Desai and I'm here with you today, talking from a small, parched village in the Mehsana district of Gujarat with a population of 3000 people. The annual rainfall here is just about 25 inches. Many years ago, a river flowed through here, and watered the crops. Today, it has dried up. Water pipes have been built, but residents get water only for an hour or so every few days. Right now, we are in the corner of Ramjibhai's groundnut field. Here I have in my hand, a single groundnut.'

Nandu extended his hand directly in front of the camera which was perched on a stand in front of him. The camera man crouched behind it. Two men with light reflectors stood close by. A picture of a groundnut filled the screen.

'Yes, it's a groundnut with the shell still on. Now I'm going to crack it open. Here we are. Now, Ramjibhai, our viewers are watching us on Television Channel 16.'

Ramjibhai came into focus on the screen. His skin was tanned and weather-beaten and contrasted with the unshaven white stubble on his chin. His mouth was crunching up a betel leaf. His scarlet and green striped shirt rippled in the breeze.

He folded his hands. 'Namaste brothers and sisters, I'm happy to be on Television Channel 16.' He spat modestly onto the ground.

'Ramjibhai, tell our audience, are you satisfied with your groundnut crop this year?

Ramjibhai shook his head. 'Arre Nandubhai, would anyone be satisfied with this?' He pointed to the shrivelled nut. 'When our river was full, our people lived comfortably, working on our land along with our bullocks. When her water was flowing on my land, my groundnuts were nice and fat. But now, see these thin groundnuts? They are from the new crop in the same field. Our small lake does not help much.

'So what happened?' The camera frame now included Nandu.

'Arre, the Lord decided it was time for change! The water level under the ground sank till our groundnuts couldn't reach it. We tried irrigation but there's not enough water. Now my fields give me only second-rate groundnuts and I get a lower price.'

'What about the others who live here?'

He shook his head and looked down. 'What can we do? Oh all our people have to bow our heads and adjust to the new situation. Now most of us also grow crops that don't need too much water. Our womenfolk are thankful if we have a well near our home.'

From the corner of his eye, Nandu glimpsed some movement. A small figure was approaching. His heartbeat changed to an excited rock 'n' roll. Maahi was here! She was coming towards them. She must have changed her mind, thank the Lord!

'Thank you Ramjibhai. May the Lord fatten your peanuts! Now tell me, is this your piece of land that we are standing on?'

'Yes. I inherited it from my ancestors.'

'Alright, then tell me, if water was found in your village, would you be able to use it to grow better crops?' Ramjibhai scratched the back of his head.

'Of course water is sacred, given by the Lord and our life depends on it. But the Lord is hiding it from us! We have wells but the water is going deeper down into the earth's stomach and it is more difficult to reach. We have dug three bore wells in the village but have not found water. A river would water our crops but will Mother Ganga spring out again from Lord Shiva's matted hair?'

For Chintu, a sudden surge of memories brought back evenings with his father, mother and Dada. Sunset colours had streamed through their square window like an expanded shimmer of holographic paper. Stories about gods and goddesses from the ancient books swirled around the room and poured into his ears. He remembered this story. Mother Ganga was to come down to the thirsty earth. Lord Shiva was worried that if she came straight down to earth, people would drown under her force, so Shiva had made Mother Ganga gentle by passing her through his knotted hair as she descended to earth.

He wished Dada was here.

He suddenly glimpsed a figure half-hidden behind Phizzy. It couldn't be... yes it was! Maahi! She had come after all! She must have struggled with herself to find the courage to come. A rush of hope and gratitude flowed through him. '*Gagdoo*,' he muttered happily. Maybe the prophecy would come true after all!

'Alright, dear viewers, we may have an answer for Ramjibhai today. Three bore wells have been dug but no water has been found. Will Mother Ganga come to us or not? Will this thirsty village find water today? Perhaps the answer lies with a young girl in this village.'

Nandu gently reached over to Maahi who was standing nervously behind Chhagan Dada.

'Maahi is her name, the name of a river. Is she a daughter of Mother Ganga?' Maahi filled the camera frame. She looked down and bit her lip and plucked at her skirt.

Chhagan Dada strode over and came into focus. 'Maybe in ancient times, but today, she is my granddaughter.' He smiled at his own joke and adjusted his *dhoti*.

'Maahi have you been living in Tintodan for long?'

Maahi did not look up. 'Four years.'

'And how long have you had this twig?'

He held up the fork-shaped piece of wood.

'A year.'

'Dear viewers, we are going to reveal Maahi's secret. She has a secret that could change the fate of Tintodan. And we are sharing it with all of you sitting in your homes watching this, here on TV Channel 16.'

Nandu waved the twig dramatically, then gently placed it in Maahi's hand.

He turned to the camera briefly. 'Remember, viewers, this is the first time we are showing this on TV Channel 16.'

He turned to Maahi and spoke softly but clearly. 'Maahi, please, for the sake of all our viewers on TV Channel 16 and for the people of your village, show us your magic.'

Maahi gave him a piercing look. She knew he was building up a drama, making the whole thing sound like a movie about aliens, where SHE was the alien. But she knew she wasn't. It was just something she could do, this water divining. She didn't even know how it happened.

Alright, she would play her part in the drama.

She took the twig and held the forked part in each hand with the end facing up. She looked at the tree stump and stood directly in line with it. Then she began walking slowly towards it.

'Watch carefully, dear viewers. The stick is an ordinary twig but in Maahi's hands it becomes a tool. See what happens as she walks. You see, she has the ability to tell where there is water under the ground though we cannot see or sense it. Now while she walks, I'd like to tell our viewers on TV Channel 16 that she is not the only one who can do this. There are others in the world like her and they are called water diviners. For some unexplained reason, water diviners can sense water under the ground through the stick. You see, the stick moves. And how do we know that the water is really there? We drill into the ground to see if we strike water.'

The moment had come.

'Watch . . . ah, look, it's started! First time on TV Channel 16!'

The cameraman zoomed in to Maahi's hands and the quivering stick.

'Can you see the twig? It has started turning! Look! It turns inwards, inwards, then down, down! Do you see that? The twig turns by itself!'

Sure enough, the twig was turning. Maahi held her hands open loosely so it was clear she was not the one moving it. The amazing thing was happening by itself.

All the people in that little circle were silent with wonder. The stick had turned even as Maahi held on to the two ends of the fork. The long end moved upwards, then pointed to Maahi and then turned downwards. It was something no one in that group had seen happening before. Maahi stood still with the stick still pointing downwards. For a brief second, she looked shyly into the camera.

'Here.'

Nandu suddenly sprang into action.

'Viju, please mark the spot! Maahi, you have worked your magic. Yes, at this very spot we shall ask Ashvinbhai Mehta to arrange his bore well machine. Ashvinbhai is a well-known pump manufacturer. He has kindly agreed to bring a super-powered machine for TV Channel 16 to test this extraordinary water divining. Thank you Ashvinbhai, how long do you think it will take for us to drill down?'

A round, pink, sweaty face appeared on the screen.

'Well, we will set up the machine immediately but it depends on how deep we have to drill. With our super-powered DTH rig, we can drill up to 250 feet in 4–5 hours.' Ashvinbhai wiped his face with a white handkerchief.

'Wonderful. Thank you, Ashvinbhai. Our viewers on TV Channel 16 will be waiting for the results of this. Meanwhile, we are going to request our young friend to show you this marvel again. Maahi, can you do your magic walk again?'

There was a general atmosphere of expectation and excitement. Against her will, Maahi too, was drawn into it. There was suspense again, as she walked, stick outstretched, until it happened again. The turning of the stick was a moment out of ancient stories, out of fantasies, out of everything that could happen in the imagination. Only, it was real and happening today, in front of them.

'Viewers, Ashvinbhai is working quickly to start the drilling. We have two special guests from different parts on India who are going to talk to us through a satellite link. Meanwhile, a quick commercial break. After that, you will be joined by my colleague Viju Patil.'

Nandu broke off and handed the mike to Viju.

'Okay guys, take it from here for the next two hours. Viju, you do the interviews with the members of the village. I'll be back in two hours. Keep me posted.' He walked straight up to Maahi and knelt down directly in front of her.

'Maahi, Maahi, I'm so sorry. I never asked you. I just thought you would want to be on TV and be a star. I thought I'd get a promotion . . . I don't know what brought you back, but all I can say is . . . *thank you*. You saved our lives.'

★★★

Meanwhile, the *pooja* had been a great success. The little packets of sugar had been distributed and lunch was being served under Dadi's supervision when Chhagan Dada left. He had come there in time to witness the water divining.

He patted Maahi's head. 'Maahi, how did you keep this wonderful secret? That was like watching a suspense movie!'

Everyone had gathered round. Maahi looked at Nandu. Then she looked down. She picked up the bundle of brown and white fur at her feet.

'We still don't know if the water's there.' She began stroking Mishty nervously.

'Don't worry, Maahi. Our viewers have seen the stick turning. Channel 16 has a good story to tell and our viewers have a story to tell their friends. If there's no water, we can interview water diviners who have been successful. Yes, we have found another diviner! Or we can say the water is too deep to drill. As long as we have shown this, we already have a story on the show. Thanks to you.'

Dadi waddled up. 'Stories, stories, let me see you conjure up potato *vada* from stories! Come here and fill your stomachs now!'

'Dadi, you are the saviour of our stomachs!' There was relief in their joking and laughing as they munched the round crisp *vadas* with their spicy green chutney.

Chintu caught up with Maahi.

'What happened, Maahi? Why did you change your mind?'

Maahi was quietly excited by the drama of the TV filming.

'Dadi says we shouldn't refuse what guests ask us to do.' she said with her hand in front of her mouth. Then she added simply, 'My father also said, "If you do what is right, the Lord gives you might" and so I had to do it.'

There was nothing more to say. The general laughter closed over them.

But the water still had to be found.

Ashvinbhai, the bore well man, was perspiring and shouting. Waving his white handkerchief every now and then, he spurred his workers on. The machine was positioned. The water would pour through the long spout. How deep was the water? Was it there at all?

The drilling had started. It was noisy but the TV crew was far enough. They would have to wait in the white OB van and watch. Nandu used the time to interview different people on TV channel 16. Chintu came on, with Chhagan Dada and Dadi. Then Vimla talked about how Maahi revealed her special talent to Chintu, and how they had contacted Nandu. Chintu was surprised at how calm he felt about being on TV. He wondered whether his friends were watching. But there were so many channels to choose from… who would want to watch Channel 16?

'Hey Nandu,' Phizzy came up to their corner and handed over the mike. 'The special people are ready to go on air. Dr Vandana Shiva is ready now. Then Rajendra Singh*ji* in 20 minutes. Time for you to take over.'

'Ok, thanks, Phizzy.' He turned to Maahi. 'And meanwhile, my little star, find some glue and stick yourself to this spot!'

The others watched as the satellite link began working.

Viju signalled for Nandu to begin. Nandu spoke into the mike.

'For those of you watching this incredible presentation of water divining on TV Channel 16, here's more. We have requested the famous environmentalist, Dr Vandana Shiva to share her thoughts on water with us. Here she is, talking to us live from her Navdanya farm in Dehradun.'

The TV crew watched carefully to see that the satellite link was maintained, while a lady with a large dot on her forehead spoke energetically from the monitor in front of them. She spoke of seeds, of farmers, of natural crops, of irrigation. 'And so, you see,' she smiled at the interviewer, 'Water is life.'

The interviewer moved on to another face.

'The Water Man of India is here too, talking to us live from Alwar in Rajasthan. He has received international awards for his work over many years. Rajendra Singh*ji*, our viewers have just seen a water diviner at work. Now that water is found here, what message do you have for us all?'

On the screen, a bearded man stood next to the interviewer. He pointed to all the land surrounding him. 'All this land in Alwar was barren. People walked miles barefoot to fetch pots of water which they had to use for drinking, bathing, cooking and washing. Now, with the help of the people and especially of the women of this town, we have been able to revive seven rivers in Rajasthan alone. In this way, we can return to the earth what we take from her. I urge all the youth of the country to do this.' He picked up a small earthen pot of water. 'So, how precious is water to us, you ask? It is as precious as ghee. I would ask all our viewers to treat it like that.'

Chintu pictured lines of women walking in the hot sun, searching further and further for water which was drying up in the heat. Chintu knew the price of ghee, the clarified butter they used in cooking. Mother used it sparingly. *Water is as precious as ghee. Wow.*

Suddenly his mouth was parched. He wandered off to find some drinking water and Maahi.

The white OB van with its round dish was bustling with people going in and out. Time passed slowly as the TV crew took turns talking. Nandu told Chintu that if the water was very deep, they may have to continue drilling for a few hours the next day too. The TV channel could not wait longer than noon the next day. Their viewers would lose interest and move on to some other channel. Besides the channel's other shows were lined up. They were all taking a risk.

'Then I will have to use all my charm to explain why water wasn't found. But we'll think of that later.'

There was some commotion in the drilling area. Ashvinbhai, impatient to find his place on the TV monitor, was driving his workers too hard. They protested.

'Eh, eh! Do you think we are your bullocks ploughing your fields, that you can goad us this way? Don't speak thick with us if you want your precious water!'

'Thick? What is thick? I am talking such easy words but if you don't understand, your heads must be thick!' Ashvinbhai retorted.

'Stop your work, fellows! We are not listening to this. Hey there, brother, switch off the machine.'

'Is this your gratitude? I get you here for a special TV show and you can't even do your job properly!'

'Okay then you take over. Do it yourself! We are not going to . . .'

His words hung in the air as a deep rumbling and hissing was heard.

Everyone turned to it as if they were drawn to a magnet. There was a moment of electric expectation. Then, it happened. A sudden cloud of dust and rubble emerged and covered the scene. Then a gush of glistening water spurted from the mouth of the spout into the hot sunlight and poured in a stream over the ground, making a trail of silver across the cracked brown earth. All their efforts, their sleepless days and nights, their desperate plans came together in that moment. Mother Ganga was upon them.

There was frantic activity. The cameraman swung over to get the machine and workers in view, Phizzy ran to get the mike. The workers had folded their hands and brought them to their foreheads in praise.

Ramjibhai cupped a handful of the new water and tenderly brought it over to Maahi. 'Drink, my child. You invited Mother Ganga here. She has come to you.' Maahi looked down. She took the water into her palms and paused. Everyone fell silent.

An elderly man in a brown kurta was keenly watching the scene. He had arrived quietly, before the water had gushed out. A slight movement from him drew Maahi's attention. She gave a cry and ran to him. She looked up at him with a small smile, and held out her cupped palms with the sacred offering. *Who was he?* The man smiled gently. He accepted the water, then looked around.

'A wonderful thing has happened here, my child. Your village has a new life and there is much to celebrate.' He looked around at the gathering. 'Mother gives us what we need. May we always accept it wisely and without greed. May we never leave her empty.' Then, in one movement, he spread his arms, sprinkling the sweet coolness over everyone around. The spell was broken.

The workers splashed the new water noisily over their faces, laughing.

Chintu stared after Maahi and the elderly man. They were talking quietly together. Who could he be?

Ashvinbhai toddled up, clasping his handkerchief and dabbing at his sweat.

'Nandubhai! Ma Ganga has been kind! The water is good, not salty!' He declared. 'Just 200 feet down!'

'Sweet words, Ashvinbhai! ! Celebrations soon. Right now let's have some action! Viju, are the cameras rolling? Let's start the audio. I'll talk. Thanks, Phizzy. Bring Maahi.'

Nandu took the microphone and breathed deeply. His face filled the screen.

'Dear viewers, the climactic moment is here! TV Channel 16 has exclusively captured the discovery of sweet water in this thirsty little village of Tintodan in Gujarat.'

He dramatically scooped a palmful and sucked it into his mouth.

'Here it is, the blessings of Ganga, our Mother! What an incredible event in the life of this village! Remember, the water was found under very special circumstances, with the help of our young water diviner. We are going to bring her to you again very soon. First, Ashvinbhai will tell us more about this remarkable discovery. Ashvinbhai, did your drill reach the water table?'

Ashvinbhai was in the moment. His shirt had big patches where the sweat had come through, and even the back of his trousers were wet. But he grabbed the mike from Nandu's hands and began. 'Namaste to everyone. I would like to introduce myself. My name is . . .'

He had found an audience and he was going to make full use of it.

Chintu had seen Maahi's face the moment the water had burst out. He had seen her staring at the spout, at the shining water and the stream forming on the ground. He watched now, as she touched the feet of the elderly man. He saw her pick up Mishty and run bare-foot towards the cow enclosure, then change her mind and disappear behind a clump of prickly bushes. He followed her now.

She was hunched up with her arms around her knees, face pressed down, rocking back and forth. Mishty pawed her and mewed.

'Maahi, you did it!'

There was no response.

'Maahi!'

When she spoke, her voice was muffled.

'It happened! It really happened!' The rocking continued.

'Yes, it happened! Maahi! Look up! Listen, everything's ok now! You did it! The water's found!'

'I can't speak. Just go now. I'll come later.'

Chintu knelt down and gripped her by the shoulders.

'Maahi, come ON now! You really are a star! Don't you see, the prophecy was true after all! It had to be someone from our bloodline and it's you! You are the one to benefit the village! You've done it!'

The rocking stopped suddenly. Maahi raised her head slightly. Her cheeks were tear-stained, but she had a curious look on her face.

Chintu squatted next to her. 'Look, it's all over now. Dada's search for the hero from his bloodline is done! Funny, he always thought it would be a man.'

Maahi opened her mouth then shut it. Then she said, 'Did you just say 'BLOODLINE'?'

'Sure! You're my Dada's brother's son's daughter. Even if you're a girl, you're still bloodline.'

Maahi's forehead crinkled for a moment. 'You told me he was looking for someone from his FAMILY. The prophecy was about someone from his family.'

'Yes, well it's the same thing, isn't it? You're bloodline family.'

Maahi was completely still. 'Bloodline?' There was silence for a couple of moments.

'What's wrong? It's true, isn't it?'

'Bloodline? Bloodline?' Then a curious sound came from her and she began shaking gently. 'And I thought the prophecy must be true! And it all happened! Oh! Oh! Bloodline!' The sound grew louder and louder. Her mouth opened wide to reveal a perfect set of teeth. She was laughing uncontrollably.

Phizzy ran up. 'Maahi, the way you keep disappearing! Come on! You're on TV. Nandu wants you NOW!'

They left.

Back under the shamiana a hundred yards away, celebrations had already begun with Dadi's food spread. Pandit*ji* had arrived in his ochre kurta, bringing a bunch of people with him from the *pooja*. Dada was slapping his neighbour on the back and they were laughing. A beaming Dadi passed out sweetmeats while Vimla handed out paper plates left over from the *pooja*.

'Glory to the Lord! He accepted our *pooja* offerings and gave us water as a reward!' declared Pandit*ji*. He plucked a *vada* from a fast-emptying plate. There was general agreement from those who had accompanied him.

'Of course the Lord's blessings are with us. But don't forget that my Maahi knew it all along, she with her stick.' Dadi uncovered a vessel filled with cool buttermilk. Vimla began pouring it into little cups.

'Oh yes, the Lord worked through her.' Pandit*ji* said, eyeing the buttermilk.

'After all, she's a water diviner! There must be something divine about her!' A member of the bunch added, while accepting the buttermilk.

Chhagan Dada broke in. 'Oh nothing divine in all that stuff! It's just a word, diviner, diviner. There are other water diviners in the world. They're all proper flesh and blood people. She's a good girl, my granddaughter!'

'But she's not your REAL granddaughter, is she? Pandit*ji* told me she's adopted?'

Chhagan Dada paused. 'Yes, my son and daughter-in-law

had no children. They adopted her four years ago when they were here. Then they moved to Ahmedabad for better jobs and Maahi stayed on here. A good child. She's just like my real granddaughter.'

Vimla was transfixed. ADOPTED? No one had mentioned this to her! If Maahi was adopted, she couldn't be bloodline! And if she wasn't bloodline, the prophecy was wrong! Then how?

They had found the water anyway! Maahi had found it. And the village would surely benefit in so many ways! Could the astrologer have just meant FAMILY instead of BLOODLINE? Even if Maahi was adopted, she was part of the family now. No. Vimla remembered clearly. The prophecy was distinctly about BLOODLINE. Was it all wrong then? Did all this just happen by chance? What did it all mean? She had no idea.

20

GOODBYES

At 4 p.m. they telephoned Dada. He had watched everything on TV Channel 16 with Chimanbhai. He wanted to know everything.

Yes, Ramjibhai would talk with the water experts to decide how the water could be diverted to help the rest of the village. The village headman would contact the water experts in the district to see the best way to use the water. They wanted everyone to get the maximum benefit.

Dada listened to everything. He was elated.

Vimla and Chintu had finally told Chhagan Dada and

Dadi about the prophecy. They had both decided they would tell Dada about Maahi's adoption only when they were back in Mumbai. The story had come out in pieces between Chhagan Dada and Dadi's recounting. Maahi's parents had lived in the neighbouring village and were distant relatives. The water in their village had become contaminated and an epidemic of typhoid had broken out. Her mother had died and Chhagan Dada's son and daughter-in-law had adopted her.

'So it was her REAL mother who was a water diviner.'

As the realization sunk in, a new feeling replaced Chintu's puzzlement about his mysterious cousin. The parents she had grown up with for six years were no longer there. He tried to think of how it would feel for him. Then he tried to shut out the thought. She was taken over by these new parents, and raised away from them, with Chhagan Dada and Dadi. Did she miss her real parents and specially her mother, with whom she had sensed water under the ground? 'Sometimes,' she had said. Was she talking about her real parents?

He understood now why she hardly spoke. He was grateful she had shared her secret with him. He was glad Chhagan Dada and Dadi loved her and were proud of her. But he felt confused and a bit cheated with the prophecy of the bloodline. And who was that elderly man she seemed to know so well?

Chintu called Arjun from the mobile phone, and received a blasting.

'You fool! It's Wednesday 6 June, the day before the competition. What are you doing there in the jungle? The project is going full speed even though it's the mid-term break, and we've been meeting every evening without you! You'd better be here tomorrow! We're going to win and I'll whack you if you miss Aamir Khan.'

'Arre it's not a jungle. Anyway I'm leaving this evening and I'll tell you everything when I come, it's a long story. But how is everything going?'

'Good. We got the boys to write and draw on the bricks on the inside wall, about themselves and water. It looks pretty cool!'

'Every class has a speechmaker to explain their project while the judges walk around.

'Wow!'

'Yup. And Principal Shashi is going mad of course.'

As Arjun talked, Chintu pictured the festive look around the school. The judges would be there tomorrow morning. Each brick of the inner wall recorded a student's personal experience with water. That was the school's water project. And here was the real water project in this faraway, dry village where water had been found in this unusual way. Arjun would be astounded when Chintu told him.

Their train was to leave that night and reach Mumbai very early the next morning. He would be there well in time for the judges. But before he left, he had to find Maahi. There were too many things left unsaid.

He found her returning in the heat from the vegetable vendor.

'Maahi.'

She stopped but did not look at him. Mishty nuzzled her leg.

'We're leaving this evening I want to give you something before we leave.'

She looked aslant at him.

'What?'

He beckoned her to the shade of the compound wall. They settled themselves in silence.

'Remember I told you about Abu Chacha near my home?'

'The one who sells coconuts?'

Chintu winced. Abu Chacha was much more to him than that, but how would Maahi know?

'Well, yes. He told me something important. But first you have to tell me about your real parents and how you were adopted.'

Maahi's face became drawn. She looked down and scratched fitfully at Mishty's fur.

Chintu waited. He could only trust that she would say something. Finally, she spoke.

'There's nothing to say. I hardly saw my father. Mother told me he worked in another town, but I found out later that he had died in an accident. My mother stitched clothes for people and I helped her at home.'

Chintu started to say something, but nothing came out.

'When she knew she could tell about water under the ground, she helped people in the village.

She glanced up at him for a brief, fierce moment.

'She never took money for it.'

Chintu blinked behind his glasses. She continued after a pause.

'The monsoons had come. One day, the village headman

announced that there was a disease going around. Typhoid. The water was getting bad and spreading germs.'

She was still now.

'Mother had fever for days, so finally I took her to the doctor and he gave her some tablets, but she got worse. I had just returned after cleaning the cowshed and stacking the dried hay out of the rain,' she paused.

'Mother was lying on the cot, her body burning with the fever. She was talking in her sleep. I gave her some water and called to our neighbours, but they were not at home. So I ran in the rain to the doctor's house a mile away.'

The scene played itself out in her memory. The pouring rain, the fear in her heart, the desperate dash to the doctor.

'He was out on a visit. I waited. He came just as the sun was coming up.'

Chintu held his breath.

'He came immediately. But by the time we reached home, it was too late.'

He could hear her quiet breathing. 'My mother was Dadi's distant niece. Dadi told her son to adopt me when my father did not return. They didn't have children of their own. That's how I came here.'

Chintu felt like his stomach had been scooped out of his body. He didn't know! All this time, he didn't know! How would HE feel, if he was wrenched away from Dada, his mother and father into a strange family he couldn't choose, into another city or town, away from everyone he knew?

He forced the thought from him before his heart began drumming again. He missed his father a lot, but after hearing

Maahi, he felt ashamed. She had just silently started a new life.

'Life is weird, sometimes,' he mumbled. What more could he say? He remembered his other question. 'Who was that man? The one you offered water to?' He looked at her expectantly.

She opened her mouth to say something. Then she closed it.

'Anupam*ji*. My father's uncle. The only one who always helped us.'

Ah. No wonder she had offered him the new water first. 'But what did he tell you later? Weren't you talking to him?'

Maahi looked away. 'He said that the underground water was like money in a bank. It's better to take only a bit at a time, else it will be finished before we are ready.' Mishty appeared from behind a bush and found Maahi's lap. She began purring. 'He can show us ways of storing rain.'

Storing rain? Water conservation? If they could store rain somehow, they could always have a supply of water. No shortage. *He could have his long, hot showers . . .* Many possibilities opened up.

'He will speak to Dadu and the elders in Tintodan,' she said quietly.

For a few moments there was silence.

Suddenly, the words tumbled out. 'Chintu, do you think this was all meant to happen? That Dadu and Dadi were unknowingly waiting for me? And my new parents too?' She looked straight at him.

'Chintu . . .' *she had said his name.* He felt a strange tingling. This was the first time she had said his name!

'Er . . .' He didn't know what to say. He couldn't believe in predictions any more. Maahi had found the water, but she wasn't from his bloodline.

'Do *you* think so?' he asked finally.

She looked up at the sky. 'I don't know. But now I have a big family.'

'Did you feel . . . like . . . strange or something? Like there was a sick, hollow space inside you?' She picked up the ever-present Mishty and hugged the brown and white ball of fur close to herself. 'Not now. I have Dadu and Dadi. And Mishty can go with me to Ahmedabad.'

They both stared at this warm bundle purring contentedly on her lap like a small engine.

'Where did you find her?'

'She just turned up as a little kitten one day. I gave her some milk. Since then she's been following me around everywhere.' Maahi tugged playfully at Mishty's ears. 'She's adopted me now.'

He remembered what he had wanted to give her. He stuck his hand in his pocket and pulled out a small smooth grey pebble with a hole into which was strung a black cord. He gave it to her.

'Here.'

She took it and turned it over between her fingers. On it, were roughly etched the letters DEB & LI.

'What's this?'

'It's a good luck charm for you. I picked up the stone near the stump of the banyan tree where you did your magic. I etched the letters into it. DEB & LI. It means Do Everything Best & Leave it.'

'What do you mean?'

Chintu paused for a few seconds to sort out his thoughts.

'Do you remember when I was trying to pull you away from the cows to take you for Nandu bhaiyya's filming? I was just trying to do my best for Dada, hoping you would find water and help the village. When you refused, I realized I couldn't force you. So I let it go. Then later, YOU realized that you had to try your water divining for the village. So you did your best and took the chance that there was water. That was more important than being scared.'

'You mean we both did our best?'

He nodded. 'Yes. We had to try. Abu Chacha told me it's important. If you do your best, don't worry about how it turns out. Just leave it.'

She turned the stone over again a couple of times, thoughtfully. Then she quickly took the ends of the cord and tied the stone loosely around Mishty's neck. She looked at Chintu. There was a small smile on her face.

'I'll remember,' she said simply.

21

BACK HOME

Chintu was surprised at how his eyes grew misty as he said his goodbyes. For the first time he was glad he wore glasses. They promised to visit each other. Maahi touched Vimla's feet and looked quickly at Chintu with a murmured 'Bye'. Then she turned, bucket in hand.

'She's a shy little thing,' Dada said. 'Not too many words in her mouth.'

She's a gagdoo, Chintu thought to himself, *a real gagdoo.*

The train jerked to a start and they settled down. They would reach early the next morning before the school competition began. And then the blow struck. There was an accident near Surat and the tracks had to be cleared. There would be a delay of several hours. They would reach late. Chintu would miss the competition.

Sitting helplessly in the crowded train, there was nothing Chintu could do. *Nothing* could be as devastating as this! He was the head of the water committee, going off to his village, abandoning his team, and finally, *not turning up for the competition!* What could be worse? He could picture Principal Shashi's green eyes flickering in disbelief and the hurt look in Miss Reena's eyes. Those hours in the train were some of the hardest Chintu had to go through. There was no one to talk to. Arjun would be in school, the competition would be going on. Nandu was still in Tintodan. Vimla informed Dada.

'Don't fret about what you can't help, Chintya. It's not your fault!' Vimla consoled him.

Abu Chacha flashed into his mind. DEB & LI again! Do Everything Best and Leave It to the Lord.

'Breathe, breathe deeply,' he told himself. He tried until he became breathless. Then he slept.

When they finally walked through the door of their little apartment, Dada hugged him tight. He looked fresh and delighted to see them. Chintu ran to telephone Arjun. It was already 3 p.m. and the competition would be over by now. No, Arjun had not yet returned from school, his mother said. Chintu wanted to go to school immediately.

'I HAVE to go! I missed the whole contest! That's the worst thing I could ever do!'

Dada turned to him. 'Never mind, Chintu. Your school day is over. Arjun must be on his way home already. Besides, you have a real reason for not being there, and Arjun will call you as soon as he can. Cheer up now!

Meanwhile, look Vimla, I have fulfilled another prophecy. I have cooked for you both today! Come, wash up and let's eat!'

They sat around the table and talked and talked until all parts of their adventure came out. They finally told Dada the story of Maahi's adoption.

'And so Dada, after all, the prophecy was wrong, because Maahi's not bloodline. What about the rest of the story? The water was found, and it will benefit your village. I can't understand it.' They both looked at him expectantly.

Dada was quiet for a while. Then, he spoke slowly. 'You're right. Maahi's not from our bloodline.' He paused. 'But the prophecy's not wrong.'

'How can you say that? Where does the 'bloodline' bit fit in? Maahi's adopted, the prophecy said bloodline, and still she found the water. I don't understand it.'

'YOU, Chintu, are from the bloodline.'

'But Dada, I didn't find the water. Maahi did!'

Dada smiled slowly.

'Hmm. Who went to the village? YOU. And who did Maahi tell her story to? YOU. Who told Nandu? YOU. Who argued with Maahi when she refused to try the water divining for the TV? YOU. It seems to me, Chintan Vishnubhai Shah, that YOU were the real trigger for all this. If YOU hadn't been there and put in all your efforts, Maahi would have gone to Ahmedabad taking her secret with her. Yes, Chintu, YOU are the one from the bloodline. This happened because of you!'

Chintu sat stock still. He had never thought of it this way. Vimla looked at him.

'Oh Lord! It may be true, Chintya! It's a different way of looking at it. I never thought of it that way!'

Before they could say anything else, the telephone rang. Vimla answered it and with a puzzled look, motioned to Chintu. 'It's for you. Kiran Rao. Is she a teacher?'

Kiran Rao? Kiran Rao? She wasn't a teacher, but surely he knew the name...

'Hello?'

A friendly, soft voice spoke to him.

'Hello, is this Chintan Shah? My name is Kiran Rao. My husband and I wanted to come and meet you for a few minutes. We are just downstairs. Is it alright if we come up now?'

'Er yes, er, we're at home. Er, who is speaking?'

'This is Kiran Rao, Chintan. Aamir and I wanted to congratulate you. So we're just coming up.'

A thunderbolt had struck. Could it be Aamir Khan and his wife Kiran Rao? Who else? But how...how? And why here?

He put down the receiver in a daze.

'Ma, Aamir Khan and his wife are coming up . . .'

Vimla sprang up. 'What? Aamir Khan? Why? Oh what shall I serve them?'

Dada had sized up everything.

'Arre don't worry, there are some hot *dhoklas* in the pressure cooker.'

The doorbell rang.

22

HAPPY ENDINGS

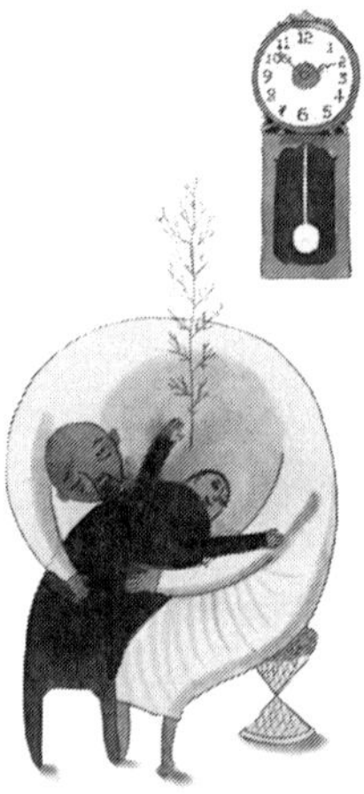

They talked about it all over the school the next day. In fact, it threatened to drown out talk of the competition itself, which the school had won.

'Aamir Khan and his wife, Kiran Rao went to Chintan's house!'

'What? Aamir Khan? Went to who's house?'

'Arre that four-eyed Chintan Shah, fifth grader!'

'That *nobody*? Why?'

'Haven't you heard? He went to his village and they found

water. His cousin's some kind of a water expert. Now the village will prosper.'

That's how the story came out, changed shape and spread. That's how most stories change and spread. By 'word of mouth', or W-O-M as Arjun put it.

Of course it all happened because of Nandu. He had called Dada, got Arjun's telephone number and told him in detail about what had happened. He told him of Chintan's role in making Maahi do her water divining. He told Arjun about how the pump had spurted water for the village. Arjun reported it all to Principal Shashi, who had passed it on, over tea, to Aamir Khan on the day of the awards. Aamir and his wife had spontaneously decided to meet Chintan. The visit had been simple, lively and quick. The last of Dada's *dhoklas* had been polished off before they departed.

In school, Chintan was slapped on the back many times and ogled at by the third and fourth graders. He wandered round the school with Arjun, amazed by the efforts that had gone into bringing in the prize. Most of all, his team's idea of the 'Wall for Water' was a decorative success. There were drawings, comments, survey reports, pledges to use less water and even a map of Mumbai's reservoirs. He was proud to be the head of this team and a bit shy too. Maybe this was how Maahi felt sometimes, when she looked down or away. She wasn't proud. She was just shy. A *gagdoo*, she was.

'Well, Chintu, we did it, didn't we! Our school's the best. By the way, Miss Reena's looking for you.' Bagadia! Of all people, Bagadia was chatting with him like an equal! Winning the competition must have done something good to him.

He found Miss Reena. She beamed at him.

'Chintan Shah, the boy who missed the competition and found water to help his village. You're just as popular now as the school. Congratulations!'

'Aw, it was my cousin. She's a water diviner.'

'Yes, one day you have to tell me all about it. Quite a story, Arjun said. But look, I called you because I wanted to tell you first.'

She leaned forward and spoke in a low voice.

'Anand Sir and I are getting engaged.'

'Oh! Wow! I mean, congratulations!'

She smiled contentedly.

'Yes, and look what he gave me as a present.' She held up her hand.

Around her wrist, hung a bracelet, with some pretty, irregular-shaped stones. They were translucent but they glinted in the sunlight.

'Remember these? The stones from his pouch! The ga... the stones you took from him to give to Bagadia.'

How could he forget? 'Oh, yes, the precious stones?'

She frowned slightly, then broke into tinkling laughter.

'Yes, precious stones. Quite precious for him.'

'It's a pretty bracelet, Miss Reena.'

'Thank you Chintan. I'll announce the engagement soon. Keep it to yourself for the moment.'

'Yes, Miss. I'm glad.'

Miss Reena looked at him. He looked happy. She ruffled his hair.

'Go on, now. Enjoy the feeling that you've won.' She walked away, fingering the bracelet contentedly.

'Hey, Chintu, what are you chewing on? You haven't

stopped thinking since you came back from the jungle!' Arjun joined him and they walked past the classrooms together.

'Hey it's not a jungle. It's just a village, with lizards and snakes and spiders and little winged insects that get into your food . . .'

'Yuck!' Arjun broke in, 'You better get yourself checked in case you've caught some jungle disease.'

'Oh come on, Arjun, it's not like that. I liked it. I was there five days, but it feels like much longer . . .'

'Yes, you ditcher! Leaving us like that at the last minute. Do you know how we fixed that huge poster? We had to get . . .'

Arjun began describing the last preparations for the competition, but Chintu cut into his description with an exclamation. They had reached the school kitchen and the compost area. An amazing sight greeted Chintu there. The compost heap had been set up and carefully covered. Vegetables were growing in Bagadia's patch; neat rows of cabbage, cauliflower, tiny tomato plants. The rusty tank was gone, and so were the mosquitoes. Bagadia and his team had done a really good job. Arjun took in Chintu's surprise.

'I'll tell you,Chintya, if Shashi Ma'am hadn't been after Bagadia's life to work on this vegetable patch, it wouldn't have turned out this way. He got a special prize for it and look at him now! All smiley and giggly . . . King Bully, Bagadia!' Chintu remembered that Bagadia had actually talked to him nicely. He must have been happy. He had worked hard to grow these vegetables.

Yes, things had turned out alright. Yet, there was a nagging feeling at the back of his head as he explored the other projects in school.

The prophecy came back to him. Was it really *him*? The bloodline? Not really. He knew it wasn't just one person who had been responsible. There was Dada, Nandu, mother, Chhagan Dada, Dadi, Maahi's parents and of course, Maahi herself. In fact, everyone connected to the whole event; they had *all* been important for the prophecy to come true.

And yet, was it meant to happen this way? Was it written somewhere on some leaf in the *Chhaaya Shastri's* bundles? How did prophecies happen? Some of them had come true. And yet, Maahi almost didn't appear on TV. She came at the last minute because she felt she had to, and because she might be fulfilling the prophecy. But then, she wasn't the bloodline person. And deep inside him, Chintu felt it wasn't him either, though Dada had explained it that way. Was he just trying to *make* it sound true? What was the real answer?

Questions and answers don't walk around in pairs like you think! Some answers come by themselves. Maahi had guessed that everything in life may not have an answer.

He remembered DEB & LI. Yes, maybe you just had to try everything best. The final answers came in unknown ways. It was like a Bollywood movie, where you never knew how the story would twist till the end. Anyway everything had ended happily.

Everything?

The ticking clock was still nagging him.

'This may be the last year of your life.'

Dada. The last part of the prophecy.

NO. Prophecies were NOT always true. This time he would take things into his own hands. He would tell mother and they would meet doctor uncle today itself. They would insist that Dada go through all the tests.

He suddenly paused as he remembered the words. ***'This MAY be the last year of your life.'*** A sudden hope sprang up. Then he pushed everything out of his mind. It was all nonsense. *Every prophecy didn't have to be true.*

That evening, at home, he was quieter than usual while his mother and Dada chatted about the other members of the family in Tintodan. He would talk to his mother that evening while Dada was praying.

There was a fumbling outside the door and a heavy knocking. Then the doorbell rang.

'Nandu bhaiyya!' Chintu ran to the door, opened it and stepped back in astonishment. A middle-aged man in a black suit with two large suitcases stood outside.

'I'm looking for a little boy with black glasses. Does he still live here?'

Dada and Vimla looked at each other startled. She ran to the door.

'Vishnu!' she cried.

'Pa!' shouted Chintu.

Dada sat heavily in his chair. He took a deep breath to speak, as the man strode in beaming.

'Yes he's still here! We all are! You rogue, Vishnu! You use my own tricks on me!'

Chintu's father parked his suitcases in the corner and touched Dada's feet.

'I'm your son, after all!'

'How? Why didn't you tell us you were coming? All the way from Dubai?'

Vimla scurried to put more food on the table. He caught her by the arm and looked into her eyes laughing.

'And give up the chance to see that shocked expression on your faces?'

She blushed and looked away.

Chintu jumped into his father's arms.

'Father, you're here!'

'Hey, hey, you're in fifth grade now! I can't be the father of a monkey anymore!'

'Oh, father!'

'But how did you get leave from your work?' Vimla asked.

Vishnu sat down and sighed. Then he stretched his legs out on the opposite chair.

'You'll be happy to know our firm has just finished the final testing for a new medicine, and I'm here to get the license so we can sell it in the pharmacies in India.'

'Which medicine, father?' Asked Chintu as he moved closer to him.

'Hmm you have the inquiring mind of a future doctor. It's a medicine which we have named *Propensolite.* It's supposed to be effective in the treatment of an illness called Haine's Disease…'

★★★

THE REAL LIFE WATER HEROES IN THE BOOK

Dr Vandana Shiva, from Dehra Dun, Uttarakhand, India, is an environmental activist who talks about the wisdom of traditional practices. Among her many achievements, she has founded the Research Foundation for Science, Technology and Ecology, which led to the creation of Navdanya, a national movement. More than 70,000 farmers, men and women, are members of Navdanya. Over 2000 rice varieties from all over the country have been conserved with their help, and 34 seed banks in 13 states across the country have been established through the work of Navdanya. Dr Shiva has appeared in a number of water-related films including *Ganga from the Ground Up*, a documentary on water issues in the river Ganges.

Shri Rajendra Singh, known as the 'Waterman of India' won the Ramon Magsaysay Award for community leadership in 2001. He brings the community together for his work in water harvesting and water management. He founded an NGO called Tarun Bharat Sangh in 1975. This NGO has helped villagers take charge of water management through the use of *johad*, rainwater storage tanks, check dams and other time-tested techniques. Over the years TBS helped build over 8,600 *johads* and other water conservation structures to store rainwater for the dry seasons. The NGO has brought water back to over 1,000 villages and revived several rivers in Rajasthan, including the Arvari, Ruparel, Sarsa, Bhagani and Jahajwali.

Shri Anupam Mishra is a Gandhian, author, journalist, environmentalist, and water conservationist who works on promoting water conservation, water management and traditional rainwater harvesting techniques. He has travelled extensively in India for this. He describes the value of time-tested systems of water harvesting in his books, *Aaj Bhi Khare Hain Talaab* (*The Lakes are still Standing*) published in 1993 and *Rajasthan Ki Rajat Boondein* (*The Radiant Raindrops of Rajasthan*) published in 1995. The Indira Gandhi Paryavaran Puraskar was awarded to him in 1996.

ACKNOWLEDGEMENTS

In His Grace.

When I was a child, my parents visited an astrologer, a *Chhaya Shastri*. After their reading was done, he turned to me and said I would write a book one day.

When I began writing, my search about water began on the Internet, with websites of facts, statistics and names. Later, in the desert of Jaisalmer, Farhad, along with Girdhariji and Chhattar Singhji told me stories.

'We *play* with water, we negotiate with it gently,' Chhattar Singhji said.

Water is a part of our family, our community, with its roots in mythology. And so Ganga came to the book not just from the matted locks of Shiva, but forming slowly, through farmers' stories, through the shape of lakes, of controlling canals, through tankers, through generations, through mystery, and through the tap. *The Water Catchers* perhaps lives somewhere between the voice of logic – a legacy from my father and the happy surrender to faith, imbibed from my mother.

This book has received much affection from many people. To all the following:

Arghyam, for the research I gained from it; Ashis Panda, on www.indiawaterportal.com who introduced me to Farhad Contractor; Farhad, Girdhariji and Chhattar Singhji, who introduced me to Jaisalmer's human and environmental ecologies; Kurush Canteenwala, whose films (*Goa Goa, Gone*, *Renukaji in Delhi's Taps*) show how 'development' can sometimes mean 'greed' blindfolded against its location and ecology; Ms J Geetha of www.gramalaya.in, who told of various ways of water divining; Ms Nafisa Barot of the NGO, Utthan, who told me about how Nature talks to us if we know how to listen; Shri Anil Chandrani, a water diviner in Vadodara, who told me about bore wells; my friend Nandini who took me into *adivasi* homes in Chhote Udepur to see the work of the Shroff Foundation; Shri Anupam Mishra for his deep knowledge of traditional water conservation systems; Dr Vandana Shiva and Shri Rajendra Singhji who had definite messages for this book; and to my loving, extended family members who were involved in some way or other with this story, along with many close friends,

I offer my deep gratitude.

And so, although *every prediction need not be true*, the book is written.